Revenant

by Zee Lacson

Editing by David Rutter
Front Cover Art by Zee Lacson
Book Design and Layout by John Lacson

Visit www.reveriethebook.com

for

my Dad,
Eduardo V. Laureola Jr
(1943 – 2006)
who was the parent that
I needed him to be.
The older I get,
the more impressed I am.

my enduring children,
Cale & Caden
who I hope to someday inspire
the same way
my father continues to inspire me.
You are the hope
I have for humanity.

my remarkable husband,
John
who always brings me home.
I am infinitely
entangled with you.

Darkness is never warm.

I blink just to make sure my eyes are open and for a moment, there is no difference. My vision adjusts slowly and when it does, they are pieces of a puzzle forming an incomplete picture.

There is a narrow paved road in neglected disrepair; the back of buildings that establishments are embarrassed to present to the public; and the faintest glow of distant streetlights gracing the alley with pity. They throw light at the back street like scraps, casting uneven shadows. The overused, overflowing dumpsters aren't as pungent as they would have been in the daytime.

Cold muffles all the senses. Even smell.

Though no amount of cold can deaden the acidic perfume of urine that had permeated the cement from all the contributions of vagrants. The product of years of combined effort is not so easily masked. My nose wrinkles in response.

Invisible fingers flick dried leaves and discarded paper napkins into the empty air, feebly trying to fill the void. My exposed ears numb from the whispering chill. I turn my cheek against the gust to avoid being hit in the face with errant refuse.

A more deliberate motion catches my eye, not governed by the chaotic tumble of wind. It is an animal cowering in the corner, covered in a patchwork of material. Its breath is rhythmic and steady.

It is a person.

I don't know whether to be frightened or curious. There is something familiar about the unfamiliarity of this. I can't shake my disquiet. I've been here before but don't rightly remember.

The howl of an ambulance siren pierces the silence and throws the muted world in a swirl of red and white. I startle at the pageant of light and sound. I look around to find the source, but it fades almost as quickly as it arrived. In its wake, it leaves a different scene.

The person hidden in the corner is awake. The lack of visible body hair makes it difficult to tell, but sallow cheeks and delicate features hint that she is a woman. A woman made older by circumstance.

Her breath is no longer steady. She sucks in air quickly and releases it through pale, cracked lips, trembling with effort or emotion. She looks right through me with eyes hallowed by the shadows.

She screams.

New World

"What the hell?"

I was swept along a wave of bouncing bedding caused by my best friend, Brieann, throwing herself on my mattress. Her hair was tied up in a high knot that was strategically messy. Soft wisps of blonde framed her face in such a way that it called attention to her blue eyes without looking like it was making any effort. This was her I-rushed-out-the-door default. It suggested that there were more important things on her agenda than an elaborate look.

It was always her agenda that worried me.

Being Brieann, she completely ignored my bed hair, morning breath, or even the fact that I was dead asleep right up to the point when she crashed on my bed. She had a purpose for being here, and she wasn't going to deviate from it. Another signature move of hers.

I pulled a pillow over my head, not to block out the light but to block out the Brieann.

"Why are you here?" I whined from beneath my shield of down alternative.

She pulled the fluffy armor off me. I dared open one eye. It was a bad idea. I was immediately assaulted by berserk enthusiasm a mere six inches away from my face. Dangerously close. I shut the eye.

Maybe she'll go away?

"How can you be sleeping?" She demanded, her melodic voice alive with outrage. It was confirmation that she had dug her tenacious heels in to stay. "*I* couldn't sleep," she continued. "And I'm not even you!"

"I'm not sleeping *now*," I complained, turning my back on her. She was just so *loud*.

She made a sound somewhere between a huff and a gnarl. "What you're not, for some reason," she emphasized, not bothering to hide her frustration. "Is downstairs talking to *him*."

Him.

I bolted upright. The allure of slumber was gone. She was entirely correct. I should not be sleeping right now. My eyes were wide. I stopped breathing.

"Now *that*," she declared triumphantly, "is awake."

I scrambled off the bed with a growl, sacrificing a pillow to the floor. She danced out of the way, satisfied by her achievement. Her calm was directly proportional to my panic. She lay on the bed smirking and watched me spiral.

I stood there for a few minutes, comically turning one way and then another. There were too many things I needed to do, and I suddenly lacked the ability to put it in proper order.

What should I do first? Get dressed? Brush teeth? Fix my hair? *Pee*?

A half a second ago, I was the main focus of her attention. Now, Brieann was pointedly more interested in her shimmer nail polish than my predicament. She watched me from the corner of her eye with studied indifference. I glared at her. It produced no effect.

"Help?" I managed to squeak.

It was exactly what she was waiting for. She grinned, swung her long legs off the side of the bed frame and pulled herself up to all her 5-foot-6 glory. She was lit with purpose. "I thought you'd *never* ask."

She then pushed me out the door, in the direction of the bathroom.

Version

The bathroom was definitely the correct first stop.

I studied my reflection under the yellow bulbs of the sink vanity. My mouth was full of toothpaste bubbles, and my eyes were still crusty from heavy slumber. It was not the most flattering image.

Get it together, London. You've got this.

I wasn't usually one for morning affirmations, but I felt that this version of me called for it.

The person I was yesterday morning was so far removed from the person looking back at me in the mirror. It wasn't the tangled mess of hair that had changed or the brown of my eyes that I had once described as "boring".

"It's hot chocolate on a snowy day," he had said in response, a few months ago. We were hiding in the park together, lamenting over things like the past, the future, and the color of my eyes.

"The coffee that wakes you up in the morning. Sweet syrup on plain, boring Vanilla ice cream ..."

I shivered at the memory of him that I had once thought was a dream.

No, it wasn't the color. It was optimism on clear display. It was a glint of anticipation and a flood of possibility. Yesterday's London was missing that. Today, that hope was strong and radiant.

I washed out my mouth, satisfied with the minty fresh feeling. I tested out a Grinch smile that did nothing to improve my reflection. It was a reflexive motion. A visual verification of that minty freshness. Oddly, it helped with my confidence.

I splashed cool water on my face, and felt the last bit of somnolence wash away with it. The excitement that had started my panic diffused into a pleasant tingling throughout my body.

By the time I was able to finally smooth my chin-length hair into its customary position behind my ears, I was smiling for real.

There was a knock on the door followed by Brieann's muffled voice. "Did you fall in?" I swung the door open. "Oh good," she continued. "You're a person again." She reached for my hand to pull me back to my room, but stopped when she saw the delicate cord of silver around my wrist. She turned my arm over, almost taking the rest of me with it.

"This is new," she accused. She pulled my wrist up to the light, straightening my elbow and sending my shoulder even farther down.

"Hey! Ow --" My protests and pain were dismissed with another twist as she pulled it closer to the hallway light. I was forced to invent new yoga positions.

"Ethan Robert," she read aloud. Then she dropped my arm abruptly because she was inclined to clasp her hands together in front of her; possibly to muffle the scream that sounded more like the high-pitched whine of a malfunctioning engine. I rubbed my shoulder.

"Did he give that to you?" she demanded.

Saying that he just gave it to me didn't do the gesture any justice. I frowned, still smarting from her forceful zeal. "No," I grumbled sardonically. "I stole it."

Unaffected by my tone, she linked her arm with mine and leaned on my other shoulder. "Like you stole his heart?" She teased. I stuck my tongue out at her, but laughed at the cheesiness of it all. She pulled me back to my bedroom.

"You didn't give me much to work with," she complained, gesturing at the outfit she had laid out for me on the bed. "I figured we should stick with classic London or else he may not recognize you."

She had matched a plain blue V-neck shirt with my favorite pair of jeans. The jeans with no buttons. I smiled at the comfortable ensemble. Up until this point, I hadn't realized that I was worried she would try to get me in a dress.

"I know make-up isn't your jam but at least put some lip gloss on." She placed a glittery tube from her own collection on my desk. "It's flavored," she added, her voice deepening a fraction to take on a mischievous tone. "You know … to add a little incentive to the next kiss." She licked her lips and winked at me.

I felt the heat rise to my cheeks, and knew that I couldn't hide the blush; so I turned my back to her. She laughed. I wasn't concealing anything from her that way either.

"So?" she asked as I got dressed, messing up the hair I had just tamed. "That's Ethan."

Ethan. Yes. The boy waiting for me downstairs. The boy, who before yesterday, was a figment of my imagination.

Or at least I had thought he was.

He had existed only in my dreams. A connection that I thought my fractured mind had made up to help me cope with reality. A secret that I kept from the rest of the world. Yesterday, he broke all the barriers. He showed up at my door, real enough for everyone to see.

The reason why Brieann was in my room at the crack of dawn.

"He's hot," she observed when I didn't respond. "I think it's the uniform." I felt the heat on my cheeks intensify but refused to acknowledge it. She was enjoying my discomfort way too much.

"Was he awake when you got here? Who even let you in?" I asked, hoping to divert her a little. She took a brush that I left on my bedside table and started on my hair. Like I was a misbehaving toddler, incapable of doing it myself.

"I don't know. I didn't see him," she shrugged. "Your Dad let me in. He was on his way out." I nodded absentmindedly, checking little boxes in my head. I remembered. He was headed to the airport to pick up my brothers.

Satisfied that my hair was cooperating, she picked up the lip gloss and handed it to me. "I'm authorized to be here. I get to be your ... chaperone!" She said the last word in a high sing-song voice, her eyes wide with delight. There may have been clapping involved. "I can't believe your Dad let him stay here. Overnight, even!"

"It's not like we're in the same room, Bree," I said defensively. She took back the lip gloss because, apparently, I was not applying it fast enough for her. She pushed my hand away, lifted my chin and started putting it on for me. I was reduced to a cosmetic mannequin head. I suppose that I should be grateful that it was just lip gloss. It could have been much worse.

"I left you alone last night so y'all can catch up and everything, but it's tomorrow now and you owe me." She cut me off with a snap of her wrist when I tried to speak, threatening me with a look. "Stay still. Or you're going to get gloss all over your teeth." Mannequin heads don't speak after all. But we can roll our eyes.

"There," she said triumphantly. "You look … decent."

She spun me around to face the standing mirror in the corner of my room. The 17-year-old that looked back at me was a much better version than the one I left behind in the bathroom.

A light mist fell all around me. I turned back to Brieann as she was tucking a small atomizer spray bottle back into her bag. The air smelled of light vanilla. I, too, now smelled of light vanilla. It was not unpleasant.

"What was that?" I asked. She shook her head and waved her hand. "Don't worry about it." She sat back on the corner of my bed and looked at me expectantly. "More importantly, spill."

I cleared yesterday's clothes off my chair, and sat down to face her. All things considered, she was displaying admirable restraint. There was so much that she thought she knew but didn't and even more that she didn't know anything about at all. I wasn't keeping track of everything but now felt guilty for keeping so many secrets from her. I realized that she had proven more than worthy of knowing it all. The full truth, not just the bits and pieces I had fed her before.

"I haven't been entirely honest with you," I began haltingly.

"I figured that much out." She waved her hands again to hurry me along. Her hands were very animated this morning.

"Let's talk slide show bullet points." She started counting off sentences with her fingers. "You are crazy about secret-service-jr.-boy-in-uniform downstairs. He's perfect. You thought you dreamt him up. You've been trapped in a long-distance relationship for infinity, making you mopey and defensive. Then you think you lose him forever, and it just destroys you." When she got to five, she dropped her hands and looked at me expectantly. "That is until he shows up with bodyguards for bodyguards to sweep you off your feet."

So maybe she did know everything. I nodded dumbly, impressed and partially terrified by her hidden powers. "How?" I started to ask.

"I have my ways," she said, not without pride. "Which brings us to yesterday, when you sent me away with Drew right when it was the best part," she accused. I laughed and relaxed.

Drew was likely the main source of her elusive "ways". Drew knew everything and in the span of that one car ride home, apparently, she now did, too. I really needed to stop underestimating her. There was so much more to her than the banal popular blonde cheerleader that she seemed back on the first day of school.

"Well, first of all, he isn't Secret Service," I pointed out.

"I saw that man's ID! It said Secret Service!" she argued.

"*That* guy was ... Ethan is not." I loved saying his name. *Ethan*. It was a simple spell that trailed threads of magic. "Ethan's a cadet in the New Zealand Defence Force."

"You weren't kidding with the whole long-distance thing," she said.

When Ethan and I first met three months ago, I thought he lived in a parallel universe that I can only access in my dreams. I thought I'd have to wait for the next life to really be with him.

The distance to New Zealand is much more achievable within this lifetime.

"You have no idea," I agreed. "He was ... hurt; so he took leave from training and found his way here."

I skipped over the part where I thought he was dead. I watched him bleed all over his weapon when he was shot multiple times, trying to save a visiting dignitary. Nor did I elaborate how he was made a hero for his efforts, and flown here at the behest of actual royalty. My emotions were still raw from the events of the past few weeks. I just wasn't prepared to go into detail.

"How long is he staying?" she asked.

"I -- I actually don't know," I admitted. I felt ridiculous not knowing but we've had to cover so much ground in just the few hours that we've been reunited. There wasn't time to really talk about everything.

Brieann fell back on my bed with a flourish. "He flew all the way around the world for you! It's like a movie!" Just as quickly, she was sitting up again. "You never said he was so romantic!"

It felt good seeing someone gush over him. It was a validation that I didn't know I had needed. I played with the silver bracelet on my wrist, hearing his voice in my head, a faint echo of what it had been last night. *"I'd like you to wear it so that you'll have proof that someone loves you ..."*

He loves me.

"He loves you," Brieann sang, voicing the thought. She was dancing around my room, the physical manifestation of all that I was feeling. I laughed again. It was a relief that I could. To be able to. I felt so good.

"You're ready," she declared, looking me up and down. "Let's go wake up Captain Kiwi!"

Contact

He was awake.

Bedding and blankets were folded neatly on the couch. There was no evidence that it had even been used. Impossibly, it looked even less used than the version of it I handed to him last night. He was standing next to the pile, just as neat in clean jeans and a crisp plain olive green shirt.

He smiled at me when I entered the room. The gold in his eyes balanced the green and was just as welcoming.

"Hi," I said in a small voice, suddenly shy. He inclined his head a fraction, a familiar motion that meant he was silently teasing me.

"Hi," he repeated, his accent hardly noticeable with so short a word. His right arm was in a sling, a souvenir from his encounter with an automatic weapon. He reached out to me with his left hand.

Contact.

His hug was inviting, comforting, and celebratory all at once. I was snared in the summation of all the moments leading up to this. As if I didn't spend most of yesterday evening in his company. As if the time and space that had separated us weren't just a matter of hours and feet.

His shirt was soft on my cheek and smelled of laundry that was both fresh from the wash and stale from being inside a suitcase. He laid his chin on the top of my head, as he does when I'm enveloped in his arms. We slid into this position easily, like putting on worn sweatpants that have already stretched out in all the right places. The rest of the world muted around us.

"And I'm Brieann," said the one person in all the world that would never allow herself to be muted. I laughed into Ethan's shirt, the moment broken.

"Good to meet you," he said overly politely to cancel out my evident rudeness. I pulled away from him and coughed.

"This is Brieann," I repeated lamely.

"I'm her best friend," she added, like I hadn't even spoken. "And I've heard sooo much about you."

I didn't know what was happening, but it didn't feel like it was good. It was that moment on the rollercoaster when you just knew things were going to go sideways. Or down. In high velocity.

"Oh, you have?" Ethan asked, taking the bait. At least one of us was going to enjoy this ride.

Brieann hurled herself down on the couch with such force that the blankets Ethan had so carefully folded slid to the floor in an untidy heap. She was either too fixated on Ethan or genuinely didn't care. I bent down to rescue the blankets. Ethan stayed in place for Brieann's interrogation.

"You're not what I expected," she admitted, cocking her head to one side and looking at him up and down. I smiled to myself. He wasn't what I expected, either. It's one of the things that I liked about him.

I piled the bedding so that I could scoop it up in one haul. "For one thing," she continued. "Your hair is much shorter than all the drawings …" The blankets all tumbled down again, this time in even more disarray. Much like the chaos in my mind. I swore under my breath. Brieann turned to me in surprise. It was like she had forgotten I was in the room, and my manifested presence was startling. Ethan was not so easily distracted.

"What drawings?" he asked.

I threw a blanket at Brieann. "Here, put this back up there, will you?" She accepted everything I was handing her. She didn't answer him right away. I wasn't sure how to feel about Brieann outing me on my art that one might consider borderline obsessive.

No, I knew how to feel. Embarrassed. That was the undeniable emotion.

"What drawings?" he asked again.

There was nothing left for me to hand her; so she looked back up at him with her full attention. I stood up suddenly. "Hey, how about some breakfast?" I asked a little too loudly. "Anyone hungry? I'm hungry." Brieann shrugged and stood up, leading the way to the kitchen. Ethan eyed me suspiciously. I grabbed his hand and pulled him along, still talking. "What are you in the mood for? Pancakes? Are pancakes OK? Or I can make French Toast. What do you Kiwis eat? Eggs? You eat eggs right? Is that better?"

He followed along gamely but the cocked eyebrow and sly grin told me that he wouldn't let this one go. After a couple of steps, he stopped suddenly. I turned back to look at him. The green in his eyes danced. He didn't break eye contact with me but spoke loudly to Brieann. "So you were going on about some drawings?" His accent was significantly more noticeable now in such a playful tone.

I heard Brieann's voice echo from the kitchen. "The ones where you have longer hair." Ethan grinned wildly.

"Oh? I liked those," he agreed. He cocked an eyebrow at me, daring me to contradict him. "Which one did you like best?"

"The close-up one, for sure," Brieann replied without hesitation. "Not the side view one but the really close up one. I think she did such a great job with your eyes. I mean, I liked the one of you leaning against the tree and the one she did where you were sitting on the grass …"

Ethan held up four fingers and mouthed out the word "four" with delighted exaggeration. His mime was louder than Brieann's voice. As Brieann continued identifying more of my drawings, he started posing like Renaissance statues. It quickly morphed into obnoxious Instagram Influencers.

Oh, he was going to be impossible about this.

My expression wasn't enough to discourage him. If anything, it only fueled his ego trip to celebrity glory. I crossed my arms and intentionally looked away, hoping it would at least slow his momentum.

His arm was around me. "I can't wait to see ALL these drawings," he whispered in my ear. The little hairs behind my neck tickled but I couldn't tell if the thrill was from his lips being so close to me or because of intense embarrassment.

"OK, Zoolander, let's see if we can feed you and not just your ego …"

Breakfast

I wouldn't have had to do much. Ethan would have been satisfied with cereal and coffee. Brieann, on the other hand, wanted to be high maintenance, and demanded Banana French Toast. Then she sat at the counter grilling Ethan about what New Zealand was like. I was busy beating eggs. How was that fair?

"Oh, make a couple more of those," she said to me as I laid out the bread. I paused, counting out the slices on the counter. There was enough for all three of us.

"How hungry are you?" I demanded. I was getting flashbacks of what it was like to feed my whole family again, and not just a couple of friends.

"I told Drew to stop by when he woke up. I'm guessing he'll want to eat too."

I've seen Drew eat. I added six more slices.

As if summoned by the exchange, the doorbell went off. Brieann acted like she hadn't noticed. "OK, so *pikelets*? What is that? Is that something you eat? What's it made of?" she asked Ethan.

"No, no," I said sarcastically, dusting my hands on my apron. "Don't get up. I'll stop what I'm doing to go get the door …" Brieann ignored me just as she had the doorbell. Ethan grinned at me before starting to answer Brieann's questions.

I wasn't genuinely annoyed, and Brieann knew it. I was loving the idea of Brieann getting to know Ethan. It solidified the reality that he was present here, in this world, and not just in the chaos of my hopeful, teen mind. I felt like the pieces of the world I had thought had fallen apart were filling in holes and making me whole again. I needed this.

Drew was rocking on his heels, hands in the pockets of his jeans, when I opened the door. He was sporting his favorite plaid green flannel open over a shirt that said: *Ew. People.* Classic Drew. I met him only a month ago at one of Brieann's parties, but he fast became one of my favorite people.

His eyes lit up when he saw me, and he broke out a big, knowing smile. I returned his smile, threw my arms over his shoulders, and squeezed. He bent down to meet my hug. He smelled of paint thinner and light cologne.

"Well, look who's come back from the dead," he laughed. I couldn't tell if he was talking about Ethan or me. I beamed at him. The statement was true either way.

"You couldn't warn me that Brieann was planning a morning raid?" I accused, making room for him to come in.

"Bruh, I woke up to a text 15 minutes ago. You had more of a heads-up than I did." He sniffed the air. "What is that? Are you making French Toast?"

"You're spoiled," I declared, leading the way to the kitchen.

"Hey," he said defensively. "It was what I was promised. If I'm expected to fraternize this early in the morning, I deserve compensation."

It explained why Brieann had been so insistent on breakfast. "Relax. Bree has you covered." She was like a scheming evil mastermind. We were all just her pawns.

Conversation actually stopped when we walked in. Drew inclined his head to greet Brieann across the room, but extended knuckles to Ethan. "I'm Drew. We met yesterday," Drew reminded him. Ethan returned the greeting with his free hand.

"Yes," Ethan agreed. "I remember." Drew then turned his attention to the chocolate chips I had laid on the counter as toppings. He started picking at it. I hit him lightly at the nape of his neck, right at the base where his reddish brown hair began. He grabbed another handful before I could take it away from him.

"No regrets!" he yelled, side-stepping me and putting the counter between us. I glared at him playfully and started the stove to melt some butter. Ethan walked over to stand next to me and just the closeness of him made me happier.

"Are you done with your podcast interview yet, Bree?" I asked, sharing an amused look with Ethan while I dipped bread in the batter.

"He has such a nice accent," she responded, talking about him, instead of to him. "I think I just like hearing him talk."

"You know he can hear you, right?" Drew asked, popping a couple of chocolate chips in his mouth. Then to Ethan, "Sorry about her. She doesn't get out much." Brieann grabbed the empty carton of eggs that I had laid aside, and threw it at Drew. He avoided it easily, sprung back into position and deliberately added more chocolate into his already full mouth. His comical expression successfully demonstrated dominance over the situation.

"Hey, hey, hey ... children ... CHILD-REN!" I exclaimed, though I didn't look up from what I was doing. I flipped slices over the skillet and smiled up at Ethan. He put his arm around my waist, and I leaned slightly closer to him.

Drew picked up the empty carton off the floor, and chucked it into the recycling bin. "Some people can be so immature," he teased Brieann. She snubbed him but had a pleased smirk on her face when she turned away.

I couldn't have dreamed up this scene if I tried. My best friends and Ethan are in the same room. Everyone is getting along. There's laughter over French Toast and chocolate chips at the start of Thanksgiving break.

All perfectly normal.

All perfectly *real*.

Meet the Family

I was about to load the dishwasher when a force that can only be generated by the assembly of older brothers blew open the door. It was followed by an alarming symphony of loud voices and unidentifiable noises.

Ethan first looked toward the commotion, then at me, taking his cue from my reaction. I sighed, then started to put the skillet back on the stove. He held up the half empty bag of sliced bread he was putting away, raised an eyebrow, and asked, "Does that mean you'll be needing this again?"

The ruckus had made it to the kitchen. Drew and Brieann leaned on one side of the counter and waved at Dad. "Good morning, Dr. Evans," they said in unison, like well-trained kindergarteners.

"Good morning, sir," Ethan said more formally. Dad waved a distracted hello to the group while I greeted him with a kiss on the cheek. He headed straight for the coffee maker.

That's about the time I was lifted up in the air and spun around. The momentum knocked over random pieces of mail and folders that had been left at the edge of the kitchen counter. It was a violent mini tornado inside our house. I would've yelped in alarm but I had the wind knocked out of me.

Not quite the magic of Oz -- just my older brother, Locke.

"London!" he yelled unnecessarily into my ear, squeezing me tighter. I was holding on for dear life, which I suppose could have been interpreted as returning his hug … if you were Locke.

"I'm … going … to … throw up …" He wasn't fazed, but he did stop spinning. He held me at arm's length and looked me up and down. While any decent human being may use this moment to compliment someone, Locke half shrugged and made a noise that sounded like, "meh". I hadn't seen him in months, and this was how he greeted me.

I hit him on the arm. "Looks like you gained some weight," I shot back. He didn't, but I said it anyway. Locke was solid but not overweight. At least not by very much. He considered himself slightly more than healthy.

He laughed and slapped his midsection gamely. "Hear that? That is the sound of peak physical performance."

"I didn't realize peak physical performance sounded like a seal clapping," I said sarcastically.

Undaunted, he responded with confidence. "That must be the applause you're hearing from all my admirers." I rolled my eyes. "This shape does not mold itself, sis. Where's the grub?"

"The two bagel sandwiches from the airport weren't enough?" A deeper voice behind him admonished. My eldest brother, Liam, dropped a duffel by the entrance to the kitchen and gave me a much more subdued hug.

Then again, a raging hurricane in Florida would have been more subdued than Locke.

"That was an hour ago," Locke complained. "It's been absorbed." He opened up the pantry and started rummaging for a snack. He would still be expecting a meal, but he wanted something until then.

"Where's Chase?" I asked, noting that the complete set of siblings was short one member.

"He's got work. He won't be able to come in until Wednesday," Liam responded. He then turned his full attention to his unfamiliar audience that were my friends. "I guess this means Thanksgiving break has started?"

"Guys, these are my brothers," I said by way of introduction. "This is Liam, and the hungry one is Locke." Locke waved a hand over his head but didn't emerge from the pantry. "These are my friends, Drew and Brieann." Then I reached over to hold Ethan's hand. "This is Ethan."

That got Locke's attention. He emerged from the pantry, his hand in a family-sized bag of Flamin' Hot Cheetos and his mouth full of the artificially colored cheese snacks. He stood in front of us. He looked Ethan up and down as he had done with me. Without bothering to swallow, he says, "Oh, so you're Ethan."

Right about the same time that Liam leaned back on the counter and said, "Ethan, huh?"

If everyone can stop saying his name right about now, that would be great.

Ethan glanced sideways at me before nodding. He was trending in my family and he didn't look like he knew what to do with that.

I didn't know what to do with that.

"Yes, and Drew and Brieann," I said again, hoping to widen the aperture of their intense focus. Liam glanced up, and gave them a cursory nod. Locke didn't bother with niceties, and just continued to chew loudly and stare quietly.

I looked at Brieann pleadingly for help. She caught on. "Did you both fly in from Chicago?" she asked. Redirecting attention is one of her many talents.

"Flew in from LA," Locke responded almost automatically.

It was the opening Brieann was looking for. "Oh! You're the brother in UCLA! That's my target school!" She now held the cookie, and Locke was her willing puppy. He abandoned Ethan, walked around the counter, and launched into discussing admission requirements with her. Well played.

That was at least one sibling missile lock averted, but Liam was still on target. "So where'd you guys meet?" he asked.

"How about we all settle in before giving our young guest here the 3rd degree, huh?" This time, Ethan's extraction came from Dad. Dad was the only other person who knew exactly how difficult it was to answer such a simple question. I was grateful for his intervention.

"Hold up! Oh, you have Dad's backing on this?" Locke said in exaggerated disbelief. "How did *that* happen?"

"Magic," I quipped, sharing a smile with Dad.

Locke snorted. "It's not magic. It's favoritism."

That was always his fallback when someone got something and he didn't. It didn't matter if we were talking about the last slice of cake or who played the first card on Uno. Sometimes the eldest got dibs. That was Liam. Sometimes the youngest. That was me. It was usually out of convenience and practicality, not to be unfair. It was only unfair in Locke's eyes.

"You've got something on your face," I said, pretending to wipe something off my cheek. Locke instinctively made to wipe off his cheek with the back of his hand, adding more red powder to his face. "Yeah, right there," I continued to bait him. "It looks like … It looks like envyyyyyy …" Locke's hand froze on his face, and he closed his eyes. The picture of a man who could not believe he just fell for an old trick.

I pretended to drop a mic and mouthed out the word: BOOM.

Liam patted him on the back, shaking his head. "Dude," he said in sympathy. Or shame. Probably shame.

Ethan didn't seem to know what to do with this glimpse of my version of family life. I would never consider my family normal, but it was more than that to him. I could see that. I knew his childhood experience was very different. He had said as much.

There was a conflict between what he knew with what he was witnessing. He was standing on the edge of his expectations, waiting for the fatal drop that he had learned would always follow. The suspicious runaway teen in him was on the surface. It was his defense mechanism borne out of years of trauma. He might have been trying to hide it, but it was there. I squeezed his hand, hoping that it was enough to reassure him. He squeezed it back, but there was hesitation in his smile.

"Truce over French Toast and bacon?" I offered to my brothers.

"Throw in some eggs and you've got a deal." Food was always a good incentive for Locke.

I fired up the stove again.

Boyfriend

"Not staying for lunch?" I asked Drew and Brieann at the door.

"Seriously? We just had *two* breakfasts," Brieann said in disbelief.

"Tempting," Drew responded. His appetite could rival Locke's. "But my mom wants me to run a bunch of errands; so I've got to go." I gave him a hug goodbye. His cologne was replaced by the smell of maple syrup.

"Want company?" Brieann offered, casually flipping her hair. She was checking her phone. "I've got nothing going on until later tonight."

"Be warned, young fledgling." Drew said in a low, forbidding tone. "I'm not talking about a fun visit to the mall here. Mom made me a list." He extracted a crumpled piece of notebook paper from the front pocket of his jeans to show as evidence of his domestic persecution.

"Still less boring than being home."

She left her car in the driveway and got into Drew's old, quirky, candy red BMW.

Dad joined me on the front step. "That kid's got good taste in cars," he said, watching them drive away. I put an arm around his waist and leaned against him.

"Yeah, I noticed that you had a 45-minute discussion with him over it."

"I think it says a lot about a person."

"Like what? Who doesn't know what a turn signal is for?" He laughed. It was an insider joke for big Bimmer enthusiasts like him. He squeezed my shoulder and looked down at me, the wrinkles on his face softened. I smiled up at him, enjoying the balance of this shared moment. It felt like we hadn't had one in such a long time.

He looked back at the kitchen where my brothers had eased their interrogation but still kept Ethan engaged in conversation. "What car does your boyfriend drive?" He asked.

Boyfriend.

The term felt strange in relation to Ethan. Not because I didn't feel committed to him, but because it felt like it wasn't enough to describe what he was to me. Yet, a confusing feeling of juvenile delight that I didn't want to admit accompanied it.

"He doesn't drive," I responded.

Dad snorted, shaking his head. "Oh, he's your soulmate, all right."

"Staaahp" I said playfully, but I was in full agreement. It was only one of the many little things that made me feel closer to him.

We walked back into the kitchen together. The boys all looked up from their discussion as we entered. "OK," Liam began, "We're trying to figure out the whole sleeping arrangement thing. Chase won't be here until Wednesday, but even then, I think he's booked a hotel."

That surprised me. "He won't be staying here? Why not?"

Locke grinned at me. "I think he's bringing a date to Thanksgiving and wants to spare them the trauma of our family." Then he looked at Ethan, "Unlike what you're doing to this poor man here."

My brothers had an ingrained ability to make me naturally defensive. "I didn't know he was coming!" I reminded them.

Locke was cavalier. "Excuses!"

I sat next to Ethan. I was still annoyed. Ethan leaned toward me. "So you'd rather I stay at a hotel?" he asked me in a low voice.

"Not what I meant!" I snapped until I realized he was baiting me. I bumped his shoulder. "Shut up." I admonished in a much more subdued tone. I was relieved that my brothers were too occupied to notice my childish outburst. Or else it would have been thoroughly exploited.

"There's an air mattress in the closet," Dad was offering Liam. "We can spread it out in the guest room for either Locke or Ethan."

"I'll take the couch," Locke volunteered immediately. "That way Liam can do his whole intense intimidation routine to the boyfriend *mano a mano*."

Before I could argue alternatives, Dad decided, "Sounds like a plan." The king had made his ruling.

I looked at Ethan apologetically. "She'll be 'right,'" he assured me, squeezing my hand. "It'll be just like being back in the barracks."

He was always good at adapting to changing situations. He may not always have coped well with it. But he adjusted. I was very proud of how he was handling not just waking up in a world very different from his own but also the additional stress of being scrutinized by my family.

Before Ethan, I hadn't ever considered what it would be like to have a boyfriend. It was cliché to assume that all pre-teen girls are scheming over boys and wishing on stars for the perfect boyfriend that will pick them up in a limo for the prom someday.

I was too busy trying to figure out how to get along with myself to even consider bringing someone else into the equation. Friendships were already complicated and tiresome. Adding all the unwritten rules of dating felt like it was the whole running-before-learning-how-to-walk thing.

That meant I never imagined how my family would react if I brought a boy home to meet them. Nevermind a boy from halfway around the world.

This felt more like parachuting with a hole in my chute.

I wasn't quite sure how to act with him around my family. It felt natural and comfortable to hold his hand. There didn't seem to be any adverse reaction from Dad or my brothers; so that was probably acceptable. But what about other things? Like hugging? Or like … *kissing*?

Where was the rule book on this whole boyfriend thing? How was I supposed to know what the line was before I accidentally crossed it?

Ethan was handling it all well, which was what really mattered here. He looked uncertain but no longer uncomfortable. He had navigated the second breakfast without needing any more assistance, though largely because Dad had distracted the hunters before they went in for the kill.

Trying not to be so obvious, I leaned shyly against him. I could smell a bit of the coffee left in the now-cold mug that sat in front of him. It was a welcome contribution to the overall ambience, grounding the memory into permanence. In his closeness, the rest of the room melted away.

"Did you sleep OK last night though?" I asked him.

"Good as gold," he assured me. "Honestly, probably the best night's sleep I've had in a minute." He squeezed my hand again in emphasis. "You?"

He was expecting a similar answer but now that he had asked, I remembered the dream that I had forgotten in the face of, well, in the face of Brieann's, as she loomed above my bed this morning.

"I had a weird dream, actually." The troubling images blew back into a swirl of discomfort and unease. I remembered the dream clearly but didn't understand anything about it. I shifted in my seat.

He raised an eyebrow. "Should I be worried?" I had dreamt about him; so what he was really asking was if I was dreaming about other guys too. He was teasing, but there was a thread of concern in his voice. I relaxed. For his sake. He had enough to juggle just being around my family.

"I do have *normal* dreams too, you know," I pointed out.

When he spoke, only one side of his mouth moved. "I doubt anything about you is normal, London." I stuck my tongue out at him.

"What are your plans today, Sweetheart?" Dad was asking. It was a reminder that the rest of the world, or at the very least, the rest of the room, still existed. I turned to face him as evidence that I was an active participant in this discussion. It was a method I learned early on in school when I was caught daydreaming instead of paying attention. When executed smoothly, I can be convincing.

"I was thinking I'd show Ethan around." I hadn't actually really thought too much into the future. This time yesterday, I didn't feel like I even had a future to worry about. Now, I felt like I wanted to do everything and nothing. It didn't matter. Both were good options as long as I got to be with Ethan.

Dad nodded, approving the plans. "Just remember that you still need to prep for Thanksgiving."

Oh, right. Shopping.

"I'm going to need the car for that," I reminded him. We were back to grocery shopping for four grown men. No, make that five grown men, myself, and whomever Chase was bringing to dinner. I was not going to be able to take home all that on a bike.

"Too bad you don't drive," Locke said.

"Meh," I responded. "That's really the only reason you're even here. To drive me around."

He emptied a bag of pretzels straight into his mouth. "It's for food," he declared. "I'm in. When did you want to go?"

I glanced up at the retro chrome kitchen clock that Dad had insisted we take from our old house. It looked like a prop from a sci-fi movie in the 60s that was trying to be modern. "How about after lunch?" I offered. "Ethan and I can get lunch downtown and meet you back here around 2?"

"Sounds good to me," he agreed. He put his hands lazily behind his head. "That gives me time to nap."

"It gives you time to help me clear the office," Liam corrected. He kicked Locke's chair. "Get up ... we've got crap to do." Locke groaned dramatically but stood.

"I'll clean up," I offered so I wouldn't be recruited into Liam's crusade.

"We've got this," Dad interrupted. "Go on with your day." It was a generous offer. I paused, unsure what was expected of me. Was this a test? Was I supposed to prove that Ethan's presence wouldn't affect how I dealt with my responsibilities?

"Yeah, go," Liam added. "Locke's got this." Locke looked from one to the other, hands spread in equal parts confusion and protest. He couldn't get a word out.

"Well, when you put it that way," I jumped in. I waved at my brothers and kissed Dad on the cheek. "Thanks, Dad."

"Me too," Locke growled on our way out. "Thank me! I'm the one that's been voluntold to clean up."

"Thanks, Dad!" I repeated more loudly, slighting Locke even more.

"Favoritism!" Locke was yelling but his grievance only made my smile wider.

Hidden Talents

I walked next to Ethan at an odd distance. Not how two people would normally walk next to each other. A little too close … touching without touching. Every now and then, I'd accidentally bump into him and felt that I had to mumble an apology.

I was clumsier than normal. Tripping over my own feet like I'd forgotten how to walk. It was different walking with someone. Not walking *beside* someone but walking *with* someone. And although we've walked together before … he wasn't my boyfriend then. I didn't know what to say or where to look.

Something happened to me overnight.

It was the California daylight. The daylight filtered everything with bright sensibility. The magical dreamlike quality of a lit night sky was what I've come to associate with Ethan. It was the everyday air that didn't coincide with the foreign atmosphere that I had thought was an alternate universe.

Walking down the street with your boyfriend shouldn't be a complicated affair, but it was. At least for me.

He took my hand after I had accidentally bumped him for the fourth time. We were two blocks away from home. He stopped walking to face me.

"What's wrong?" he asked. He always tackled things directly. I bit my lip. Not because I didn't want to tell him but because I didn't know how. It sounded stupid and shallow. After everything we had gone through, this seemed like such a trivial thing.

"Is this weird?" I asked. He didn't answer. He simply lifted an eyebrow. He needed more to go on and waited for me to elaborate. "I've never had a boyfriend before," I admitted. His expression softened, and a very gentle smile pulled his lips together.

"Everything is different," he agreed. We started walking again, but he hadn't let go of my hand. This was better. Much less awkward. It always felt better when there was actual contact.

"I've seen American TV, you know? I thought I'd be more prepared." There was amusement in his voice, a much lighter emotion that I'd have had in his place. "Everyone speaks different. Everything *smells* different. Even the light looks strange. It's like I'm *in* American TV and I don't know the lines."

He was freaked out. He just hid it better. I squeezed his hand.

"I've never been in a real relationship before either," he continued. "I don't know what's supposed to be normal. I don't know how to act."

Having him admit that actually made me feel better. I leaned up against him and we fell comfortably in step. Walking in unison with significantly more ease.

"Do you think they like me?" he asked with a vulnerability I didn't recognize in him. When we had first met a few months ago, he was the most guarded individual I'd ever met. Just looking at him felt like I was looking at layers on layers of emotional casing. He wouldn't answer a single question with any straightforwardness. I accepted that he was just wired differently.

Here he was, stepping out of his casing. He had one arm in a sling, the other holding my hand. He was looking for others' approval. He was risking something. He was telling me that I was worth that risk.

"My friends are all over you, for sure," I assured him, swinging his hand with mine. I liked how that felt. "But, clearly that doesn't take much," I joked. "Like, apparently, all you need is an accent."

He was looking down at our feet as we walked but he was smiling. There was a boyish charm to his smile that melted my heart more. I was glad that made him happy.

"I honestly don't think my family knows how to react either. Dad seems to get it. More than anyone can. But he also has to be, you know, a dad." I shrugged. "My brothers are a little thrown off too, I think. Since I'm the only girl in the family, I feel like they've been indoctrinated with the idea that as older brothers, they have a duty to give you a hard time."

A squirrel ran in front of us, stopped for no apparent reason, then ran up the tree it came from. I wondered if there were squirrels in New Zealand. If this was as strange to him as it had been for me in the forest where we met. The roles have been reversed. He was on my turf now. The *wop-wops* of suburban America.

"Liam had a girlfriend a couple of years ago," I mused. Kourtney had joined the family for dinner a few times. She was polite enough. Even with that annoying high-pitched voice that Locke and I had made fun of quietly in the other room. Dad was cordial and welcoming.

In fairness, I think she was trying her best to befriend me. I certainly scored expensive presents during their dating tenure. I didn't set out to dislike her. There was something about the way she treated Liam that I didn't like. It didn't feel right. Whenever she was around, Liam acted strange. He was always concerned about her but she didn't seem to really care how anything affected him. I decided that she didn't respect him enough. They dated for two years. We were always nervous that they'd actually end up together.

"I hope this isn't payback for him."

"Hey," I protested. "It's not like I really *did* anything." True, I was relieved when they broke up. I celebrated quietly with ice cream that night.

"I'm sure he could tell that you didn't approve," he insisted. "You have more power than you realize."

We had made it to the park entrance near the town center. The smell of sage was stronger when we approached. Magenta flowers peeked out of blue green felty leaves. Tall trees lined a cemented walk path. Just enough to provide shade. Their deep green leaves fluttered a greeting with the breeze. The fact that flowers were still in bloom and the trees were filled with healthy green leaves made the whole scene unrealistic. Even more than having Ethan here next to me.

Having lived in Illinois for all my life, I looked forward to the dependable changing of the season. It was a routine that marked the beginning of the end of the year. The colder air meant layers of clothing and the falling leaves meant walks were satisfyingly crunchy.

Here, it meant rain. And rain only made the green even more green. This may actually have been more familiar to him than it was to me.

"I didn't like her very much," I admitted.

We stopped by one of the empty benches. Instead of sitting, I turned to face him and said simply, "Kiss me."

It was probably not what he was expecting. He was undaunted by the challenge. His sometimes gold, sometimes green eyes were bright in the early afternoon sun. He searched my face, looking for the answer to a question that he hadn't asked. His lips parted ever so slightly, stretching into a smile.

I waited, memorizing everything about him at that moment, so different in the daytime than last night under the stars. Yet also so familiar.

He did kiss me. Softly at first and then with a little more intensity. I put my arms around his neck, unwilling to let him go.

When he finally broke the kiss, he touched my forehead with his and rested there for a moment. "See?" He whispered. "Powerful."

Einstein

"How long can you stay?"

I finally had the courage to ask. We had made three laps around the park, walking hand-in-hand, occasionally kissing. There were college kids playing football in the field, young parents pushing children in strollers, and bikes everywhere. It was a small enough town but we didn't bump into anyone I knew. Probably because I've only lived here for three months. We settled down on one of the empty park benches facing a small fountain.

His hand tightened around mine for the same amount of time that he was holding his breath. He relaxed his grip when he spoke. "I'm supposed to stay a week …"

A week?!

That was when Einstein's Special Theory of Relativity made sense to me. Things like awkward puberty conversations with your parents; waiting for your phone to charge; or the final period on the last day of school. These were slow and painful events that made time linger just to torment.

A week with Ethan was a flash of time in comparison. A week wasn't enough time to catch up on the many experiences that we were missing. A week was less time than it took for the scar on my arm to heal. I couldn't even binge a season of *Star Trek* in a week. A week was suddenly just a quick bathroom break in the roadtrip of our lives.

And we've already lost a day.

"And then what?" I asked, letting go of his hand. His jaw tightened imperceptibly. I'd have missed it if I wasn't looking directly at him, watching for his reaction. His fingers twitched. He was spinning a non-existent knife in his hand. It was further evidence of internal conflict.

"I'm supposed to fly back. I mean, I can't report for duty or anything yet, but I only asked for a week."

"What? Why?"

He ducked his head in a gesture of apology. "I didn't know what it was going to be like coming here. I didn't know if I'd even find you. I didn't know if you'd even want me if I did. This was, at best, a shot in the dark." He stumbled over his words, reluctantly sharing feelings. He looked away. "And if everything went badly … I didn't want to stick around."

I realized how insensitive I was being. Ethan had plenty go badly for him in his life. I met him in a dream. I had a fever-induced seizure that apparently had sent a materialized version of my consciousness to the middle of a New Zealand woodland. I had never been to New Zealand before … technically, I still haven't been. But that's where I met Ethan.

He had been alone by design. So traumatized by past betrayals that he preferred solitude over disappointment. It was safer.

That changed when he joined the military. It was a metamorphic experience for him. He rose to every challenge. He applied himself. He made friends. He stopped running away.

Then just as quickly, things went badly again. It took less than a day for his new life to come crashing around him. An afternoon of terror. He's had to fire his weapon. He's had to use his knife. He's had to watch some of his new friends die.

He lived. They died. Even when things go right, they also go wrong.

I had been so selfish to not see it as one more souvenir added to his collection of mounting distrust in the world. Another stab of painful memories added to a lifetime of painful memories.

"I'm sorry," I admitted. "I wasn't thinking. You've gone through a lot ..."

He waved his hand in front of his face like he was swatting away a fly. "Stop. No. Just stop." His words were clipped with sharp impatience.

I stopped.

He still wouldn't look at me. He clenched and unclenched his hands. He was working through something but didn't have the words to say what it was. Or he just didn't want to.

"Are you OK?" I asked.

He closed his eyes. His fists stayed clenched. He didn't answer.

Of course he wasn't OK. I didn't know what to say. He was hurting, and I didn't know how to help. It was impossible for me to understand what he was going through. There were very few people who could.

It had all been just a dream to me; so it was easier to detach myself. Ethan had always felt real; everything else felt far away. Almost like it never happened. He didn't have that luxury. There was no distance that could take him far enough away from what happened.

I may not even have what he needed. I just wanted him to know that it was OK to not be OK.

"Talk to me?" I offered.

He opened his eyes. His smile was forced. "I'm not sure how."

Internal conflict roiled beneath his very steady exterior. I had been so caught up in the excitement of his presence that I didn't see it. I rested my hand lightly on his fist. He looked at me.

"I'm here for you," I reminded him.

He pulled me close so that our foreheads were touching. I closed my eyes. I could feel the heat from his breath. He was pulling me into his bubble, sharing his unspoken emotions through physical contact. There was anguish and anger in every exhale. I could feel it. I fell into the moment.

I didn't know how long we stayed that way, sharing a space together. Time was forgiving. It stretched the present, allowing us to take what we needed from it. Like a slow leak, the tension seeped away until he was unclenched. He was saying plenty without uttering a word.

"Thank you," he mumbled finally. "It means a lot. Really, it does." He pulled away so he could look at me. His eyes, more gold than they were green at that moment, harbored unshed tears. He had closed the gates again but first let me visit for a moment. "It helps," he assured me. "I'm just not ready to talk about what happened yet."

It wasn't up to me to tell him how to handle his grief. It was not always easy to find a stable place to stand in the wave of such raw emotions. Sometimes, it was too much to confront. I get that. I put a hand to his face and he kissed it.

"I don't want to spend my time here that way," he insisted. His resolve was real though delivered as gently as possible. He was the one hurting, and he was still trying to protect me.

"How did you want to spend your time here, then?" I asked. I would follow his lead.

His mood instantly lifted. This time, his smile was playful. "I have some ideas."

"Oh, really?" I welcomed the return of his good mood. "Like what?"

He kissed me, the smile still playing on his lips as he did. How can there be so many ways to share a kiss?

"I like your ideas," I admitted.

"I have good ideas," his voice was low. He had relaxed. The haunting emotions that I had resurfaced with my thoughtlessness didn't linger. He chose not to dwell on them. I couldn't say if that was the best way to handle the situation, but I wasn't qualified to decide anyway. The best I could do was be there for him when he was ready to confront them.

"It seems that things aren't going too bad?" I asked hopefully.

"The opposite," he confirmed. He took my hand and brought it to his lips. "It's very, very good."

"So you'll stay!" I concluded.

His expression wasn't as positive. "It's not that simple, London. There are regulations … procedure … the whole lot."

"You're a national hero!" I protested, letting go of his hand. "You should be able to get anything you want!"

He laughed without humor. "I don't think you have a very clear idea of how the government works." I pouted. He lifted my chin gently so that I'd look at him. "They did actually bring me to you, remember? That's national hero stuff."

I knew he was right. It was no small feat that we were finally united. It took sacrifice. It took royal interference. It took Ethan getting shot.

It just didn't feel like it was enough. The scales weren't balanced. I sat back on the park bench feeling cheated.

"Look how far we've come," he insisted. I looked at him reluctantly. There was a twinkle in his eye. Wasn't I the one trying to console him a moment ago? It was laughable how quickly our roles reversed.

"Do you remember the last time we were complaining about the unfairness of our situation?" he asked. "Except back then, I thought you were an angel, and you thought you came from a parallel universe." In spite of myself, I smiled. "I'd say this was an upgrade."

I sighed. Again, he was right. I hated that.

"I wonder," I said, sitting up. "If I can still find you that way."

"With candy?" He was teasing but a light frown shadowed his good humor.

"No, I mean when I'm sleeping. I don't know why I didn't find you after you got shot but now that I sort of know how it works, maybe I can find you again." It made total sense. "Who even needs a plane ticket?" I grinned, literally sitting at the edge of my seat.

Ethan was troubled. "How does it work? Didn't you have to be sick for you to do that?"

"If that's all it took, I should've been able to find you when I was in the hospital, but I didn't." Admittedly, that put a damper on my brilliant plan to beat this whole long-distance relationship obstacle.

"So …" he prompted. "Why didn't it?"

Good question.

The truth was, I didn't know how anything worked. Not even sort of. I slammed my hands on the bench and threw myself back in a tantrum. He raised an amused eyebrow. "And you think it's unhealthy that I play with knives," he admonished.

I stuck my tongue out at him.

"We've come so far, and I still don't know how this … this …" I didn't know what to call it so I was reduced to undignified hand flapping. "… *thing* … works!" If I couldn't even identify it, how could I presume to control it? It was all so frustrating.

He reached out for my hand and brought it to his lips again in a soothing kiss. "It brought us together," he reminded me. "Nothing else should really matter right now."

I frowned, still unconvinced. "Look," he insisted. "We found each other when we weren't even looking … across parallel universes, we thought. A little distance isn't going to beat us."

There was that certainty again. It was contagious. I leaned toward him for another kiss.

"And I'll pack my pockets with Pascalls if I have to," he whispered just as my lips touched his.

Intermission

Shopping didn't happen. Ethan and I spent too long at the park. I blame Einstein. But even if we had gotten home earlier, it wouldn't have made a difference. Shopping didn't happen because by the time we did get home, Locke, our designated driver, was "napping off the jet lag".

Jet lag. From a flight that took all of one and a half hours.

Liam offered to take us, but that was ridiculous. He had taken the red eye flight, which meant he spent the night in the Denver airport just so he could get here this morning. He was exhausted and should have been the one sleeping it off. Instead, he was running on unhealthy doses of caffeine.

"I'm not cooking tonight," I announced. "There'll be plenty of that on Thursday."

Dad and Liam were sitting at the kitchen table. Liam was nursing what would've been his sixth cup of coffee by my count.

The dark lines under his eyes were like rings on a tree. You can tell how long he'd been staying up by how much they sagged. It made him look so much older than he was. It was his properly styled hair and pressed shirt that saved him from looking like a tired middle-aged Uber driver working the night shift.

Dad was leaning back on his chair with a red pen in his hand. There was no paper on the table. He rubbed his free hand over his thinning hair as he often did without thinking. He looked up to acknowledge me.

"What are we doing for dinner then?" He asked matter of factly. He wasn't being passive aggressive. He genuinely wanted to know if I had a plan.

I did not. I considered Ethan's incapacitated arm. He needed something easy to eat. "Burgers?" I suggested.

Dad looked at Liam. Liam shrugged. "Sounds good to me. Double bacon cheeseburger," he ordered. "And cheese fries."

"It's 3," I reminded him. Surely, he didn't mean that we needed to eat now. It was sometimes hard to tell.

"It'll probably be 5 when Locke wakes up," Liam countered. "Have him take you. That way the food doesn't get cold." I rolled my eyes. Locke can be such a baby.

"Did you at least get the office cleared before he crashed?"

"Oh, yeah. He brought Ethan's stuff to the room already. Do you want to show him where he'll be tonight?" I nodded and gestured for Ethan to follow me to the ground floor bedroom that Dad used as an office.

"He's still not allowed in your room," Dad called after us when we left the kitchen. Cringeworthy.

"Yes, Dad," I yelled back. "I knooooow."

"How am I going to see all those amazing drawings of me that

Brieann was talking about then?" Ethan asked in mock dismay when we were out of earshot.

"Maybe they don't exist. All theoretical. Alleged drawings." I shrugged. "You may never know."

He grabbed me around the waist and pulled me back to him. The wide leather band of his watch dug into the small of my back, but I didn't mind. I let out a little yelp and laughed. "Oh really now?" he asked. His grin was playful, and his hazel eyes were equally impish.

"Yeah," I challenged, still laughing. "What are you going to do about it?"

"I dunno about him, but I may puke." Locke announced from the doorway. Ethan let go of me immediately and I almost fell backward. Locke was leaning on the wall with his arms crossed and making vomiting noises.

"Mature," I admonished, mildly annoyed by the interruption. He made one more choking noise; then winked at me.

"Come on," he said to Ethan in an overly friendly voice. "I'll show you where you'll be sleeping tonight." Locke threw his arm around Ethan's shoulders and intentionally pulled him further away from me. Ethan let him. I stood there, my hands on my hips, fuming at my brother. He used to be my favorite. He was quickly falling down the ranks.

When their backs were turned, Locke looked back and winked again.

Yeah, I think he's my third favorite now. Out of three.

Burgers and Ice Cream

Burgers were not my favorite. For the first 16 years of my life, it was one of my least favorite foods. I'd always opt for a chicken sandwich instead. Or nuggets. Anything but burgers. I just couldn't understand all the hype. As far as I was concerned, it's pizza over burgers any day.

Two summers ago, Chase took over the grill in the backyard and cooked up the best-ever homemade quarter pounder burgers stuffed with bacon and covered in melted cheddar cheese. He served it up in warmed pretzel buns on a bed of fresh lettuce, onions, and tomatoes.

I ate two of them. And a half. Then I hoarded another two to eat later.

It turned out, It was just lousy fast food burgers I didn't like.

Chase didn't cook for the family very often; so even if he were here, he probably wouldn't be volunteering. Fortunately, our local restaurant, *Caden's*, made quality burgers. That meant that even if we couldn't have any of Chase's grilled masterpieces, we still had a pretty great dinner.

Burgers meant that Ethan could eat one-handed without difficulty. Dad and Liam were easy enough to please when it came to food. They were hardly ever a problem. Locke's issue was more of quantity over quality. As long as there was enough food, we were good. We ordered three double cheeseburgers with everything on it, cheese curds, chili fries and a shake *just for him*. I would hope that we were all good.

I looked around the table and smiled. It had been too long since I've had dinner with even just one of my brothers. Here we were, most of the family sitting at the table over burgers and fries. And while I'd prefer that Chase be with us to complete the circle, it was still reminiscent of so many dinners in my life. Except this time, Ethan was next to me.

It was the perfect mundane end to a day that still felt like it couldn't possibly be real. I released the hidden tension in my shoulders. I allowed myself to be happy in the moment. I took a long sip from my root beer float, and felt a sharp pain in my head. I must've made a noise because it caught Ethan's attention right away.

"Brain freeze," I explained, feeling the aftermath and slight buzzing that lingered.

"Drinking problem?" Locke asked. I stuck my tongue out at him. He took a deliberate longer sip from his shake until all that was left was the loud slurping sounds of air bubbles. Then he burped. "That's how it's done, rookie," he chided.

Instead of dignifying that with any kind of response, I picked up discarded wrappers and empty bags off the table to toss them in the trash. "Wanna catch some American TV, Ethan?" I asked.

"Oh, is this the whole Netflix and Chill that young people keep talking about?" Dad asked. Liam chuckled. Locke snorted. I made a face.

"Ew. Gross, Dad."

"You do realize that we get American shows back in New Zealand, yeah?" Ethan asked with a smile. I narrowed my eyes at him. My brothers were both grinning.

"I don't know if I should be happy or irritated that you're fitting right in with the family," I complained.

"Sucker for punishment," Locke proclaimed. "You must miss us so much."

Ethan stood and started to help me clear the table too. "Suckup," I accused him, but I accepted his help. He was too cute for me to stay irritated. "OK, so no TV. What do you want to do then?" I asked.

He cocked his head to the side. He hadn't given it much thought either.

As much as I enjoyed having dinner with the family, I wanted more alone time with Ethan. "Did you want to walk around downtown?" I suggested. We had the best conversations while we walked. He smiled his approval. I looked over to Dad for permission.

"Just come home at a reasonable time," he said. "Like 9 or something."

"I'll come with," Locke said, also getting up.

"I don't need a chaperone," I whined. "Why does everyone suddenly want to be around?"

"It's not all about you, you know," he replied. He crumpled up the last of his sandwich wrap, and did a free throw for the kitchen garbage can that I still had open. It went in. "I saw an ice cream shop somewhere on the way to burgers. A man needs his dessert."

"You literally *just* finished a large shake!"

"That was my drink … not dessert."

I grabbed my jacket just as the doorbell rang. Brieann was back to pick up her car. I was just in time to see Drew drive away when I answered the door.

"I thought you picked your car up hours ago!"

"That was the plan, but the day sort of got away from us. His mom insisted on feeding me." I had heard delicious rumors about Drew's mom's cooking; so I couldn't blame her.

I left the door open for her to come in if she wanted. "We're just heading out for dessert," I told her. "Locke wants ice cream."

"Oh, that's perfect. I'm meeting Tristan and E at *The Shoppe* right now. I think Raven is coming too. She and E are a thing now or whatever. Want a ride?"

I let Locke sit shotgun so that I could sit close to Ethan in the back of Brieann's Volkswagen. Locke was never awkward. He got along with everyone without even trying. He slid easily into the front seat and started talking to Brieann like they had been middle school friends. Brieann was a perfect match for his extrovert tendencies. Their conversation was comfortable and animated. More importantly, it didn't require any input from me. That gave Ethan and me a semblance of privacy.

It was nice knowing that I wouldn't wake up from this dream at any given moment. Or be yanked from the scene as I had before. However, it was tempered by the reality that our time together had a deadline.

Ethan wasn't really in the mood for dessert, and I wasn't in the mood to socialize. Locke walked into the brightly lighted ice cream shop, *The Shoppe*, with Brieann to meet her friends. Ethan and I found a wooden picnic table outside to sit together. We sat on the table with our feet on the fixed benches. As long as you weren't sitting on something sticky, it was just more comfortable that way.

"Are you an outcast, or do you just like to play one for my benefit?" he asked.

"They're Brieann's friends, not mine." If it had been up to me, I wouldn't be hanging out with any of them. Brieann just didn't leave me much choice. "I don't really know any of them that way."

I felt guilty for having less-than-favorable thoughts about them; so I thought an excuse out loud would balance the scales. "I've only been here a few months; so I haven't really had lots of opportunities to connect or anything."

"How long have you known Brieann?"

"Well, actually, I met them all at the same time."

"Yeah?" He was mildly surprised. "Seems like you grew up together or something. You have that whole best-mates-since-you-were-both-a-couple-of-sprogs vibe going on."

I watched Brieann through the oversized windows of *The Shoppe*. Tristan had his arm around her, but she was more engrossed in conversation with Raven. The overhead artificial lights were bright all around them but she was slightly more well lit in my eyes. Yes, without question, she was my best friend. At least one of them. She and Drew had carved their own safe niches in my life that I just accepted without question. "Is that strange?"

"That you have an obviously deeper friendship with someone you've known for only three months?" he asked with irony. I didn't pick up on it.

"Yeah. I mean, if time is what makes a friendship, how come she's my best friend when I've only known her for such a short time? That's not normal, is it?"

He was looking at me with a half-smile. His eyes sparkled with mischief, and I couldn't figure out why. I looked back at him questioningly. He waited, and didn't speak.

"What?" I finally demanded. He laughed.

"I'm in love with you, London," he said plainly. "It may not have been love at first sight, but it was definitely damn near close when I saw you the second time." I smiled at his admission and rewarded him with a light kiss. "It was the floss," he added. "You looked like such a happy little Pygmy Shrew munching along ..."

"I don't know what that is, but it had better be an adorable looking creature," I warned him. He laughed. "I swear, if I find out that a Pygmy Shrew looks like a blobfish or something, you are in so much trouble!"

He pursed his lips and started making fish noises. I lunged at him. He caught me with his free hand and leaned back. We almost fell off the table. "Ow! Gunshot wound, remember?" He protested, laughing. I sat back up reluctantly. I put a hand gently on his shoulder to tell him that I was sorry, but my ego refused to say the words. He put one hand over mine in silent acknowledgment of my apology. Then he took my hand and kissed it. Always the gentleman.

"It's not time that determines a connection between people," he said still quietly. "Time just provides the opportunity to strengthen it."

The stars were high in the sky. It was a beautiful, clear night that marked one less day with Ethan. Our time together was running out and with it, the very limited opportunities to strengthen our relationship.

Limbo

The stars seemed different. Mostly because they were obscured by the tall buildings around me. California didn't have tall buildings. Tall buildings didn't fare well with occasional earthquakes.

I was somewhere else.

I've been here before. I've done this before. The little hairs on my arm prickled. I didn't want to know if it was because of the unusually chill air or because of fear. I tugged the notably insufficient hoodie tighter around me. I felt the temperature through my thin jeans and classic Chucks. A gust of crisp wind hit the back of my neck and threw my hair over my eyes, momentarily blinding me.

I already knew what I would see. I jerked my chin up and toward the wind. My hair flew out of my face, exposing my ears to the cold.

And sure enough, the figure was there. I expected this so I didn't recoil at the sight of her.

I had seen many homeless people in my life. Some were a product of bad decisions, others of just bad luck. No matter how they got to this point, they were still people. Dad always told me to treat them with respect and a couple of volunteering stints at the food bank had taught me why. Being homeless was a temporary situation. Sometimes, we could all use a little help to make it through the ugliness. Sometimes, all it took was being kind.

All things considered, there was still something very different about her.

For one thing, her completely hairless, thin skin was not normal. It was a sign that something wasn't right. Her complexion was pale, almost like she was tipping between being solid and fading in the background unnoticed. Like a misaligned screen protector on your device.

She hadn't noticed me yet. It gave me time to scrutinize her.

She had a faraway look in her dark eyes. Though she wasn't looking at my direction, she was looking well past what was in front of her. What I had thought was an uncoordinated pile of material on her was just a knitted shawl. The different-colored yarn gave the appearance of patchwork. Mostly shades of violet. It was wrapped around her neck and shoulders like an oversized scarf. That seemed to be her only barricade against the elements. The flared jeans she had on may help but the very thin sweater under the shawl provided very little protection. She was huddled in the corner, her knees to her chest, in a failing attempt to stay warm.

She was the same woman I had seen before. The one that screamed at me.

I stood there, unmoving, watching her blink and breathe. Five minutes passed. Or two. Maybe it was just one. Time didn't make sense when you were freezing. I waited, expecting the sirens again. I waited, preparing myself for the scream that was sure to follow.

Nothing happened.

I rubbed my hands briskly together, encouraging circulation. I exhaled slowly into them and felt the heat from my breath spreading through my fingers in temporary relief.

My movement caught her attention. She jerked her head in my direction. There was a mad look on her face. It wasn't a constant expression but more like a quick succession of continually changing emotions. It was like her brain was surfing the Netflix menu for something to watch.

I stepped back, aware that this wasn't the safest of circumstances. Crazy followed its own set of rules. And she was probably sick. What disease causes you to lose all your hair? More importantly, was it contagious?

She didn't scream this time. She scrambled to her feet, uncoordinated and clumsy. She stuttered as she moved. It was both guttural and piercing. Not at the same time but alternating. I couldn't understand her. She took a step toward me but stumbled. She hit the ground with one knee and sprawled forward with one arm outstretched.

It was distressing to watch. Instinctively, I stepped toward her and knelt, still careful not to touch her.

"Hey, are you OK?" I asked.

She looked at me but it was as if she wasn't seeing me. She was looking *through* me. "Help," she begged in a raspy voice. Her voice sent chills to the back of my neck and not because of the wind. Her hand was shaking when she reached for me. "Help my baby."

Then she grabbed my arm with a cold, pale hand.

Somnolence

I bolted straight up in my bed, shivering.

I wasn't in my hoodie or jeans. I was in lightweight flannels and a tank top. The sleepwear I've adopted as a uniform for the majority of this past month. Both pillows I liked to sleep with migrated to one side of the bed and my sheet was tangled around my arm.

I knew I was dreaming just then but I was still startled to be pulled out of it so forcefully. I felt my heart beating in my chest. It was like the end of a particularly torturous gym class. Without the smelly locker room.

I swallowed a few times, trying to catch my breath.

I unwrapped my blanket and rearranged my pillows. It wasn't particularly cold, but I was still shivering. I had probably been lying over my blankets for the past few hours without realizing. The silver links of the delicate chain that Ethan gave me were cold around my wrist. I pulled both the blanket and comforter up to my chin, and tucked myself in. I fell back into the bed with deliberate force. The pillow caught the back of my head and expanded around my ears like a contained splash of fluff. The mattress gave a little but bounced back into position. There was something satisfying about it.

I stared up to the ceiling seeing the haunting image of the hairless silhouette of a person rather than the smoke detector that was installed there. I hadn't realized that I was unconsciously rubbing my wrist, where she had grabbed me. I still felt the ghost of her frighteningly cold hand.

I shook again, but more to rid myself of the memory than because I was cold. I was almost afraid to go back to sleep.

I smiled at the thought. Not because that was particularly amusing, but because it reminded me of the last time I was afraid to go back to sleep. Back when it was still Ethan I was dreaming of and not some mental crackbrained ghost. I had been afraid of the effect I'd have on him. I was afraid that being with him would somehow also destroy him.

It didn't, of course. I had overestimated my influence.

Losing him almost destroyed me. He had found me despite the odds. At that very moment, we were even under the same roof. All was well. At least for now.

I closed my eyes and willed my body to unclench. It was almost impossible to relax and not feel so vulnerable at the same time. Every time I felt a muscle soften, another would tighten in anticipation. My body was fighting sleep, probably because my mind didn't want to end up in the same dream again.

Don't think. Don't think. Don't think …

It was supposedly a tried method to fall asleep. The military method of counting sheep. Maybe it only worked for the military.

Maybe it only worked after a hundred push-ups and countless miles of running.

Thinking about the military led me to think of Ethan in his uniform. The first time I saw him when I wasn't dreaming. I remembered the solace and hope that flooded the sad hull of a person I was without him. It was magic.

I smiled, feeling that same rush I had felt that evening and before I knew it, I was asleep, dreaming of happy memories instead of creating new nightmares.

2nd Breakfast

"Finally," Locke declared with a mouthful of cereal. He had his phone in one hand and a spoon, dripping with milk, in the other. "I thought you'd never get up."

It was a little after 10. I was up 15 minutes prior but thought it would be good to freshen up and get dressed before heading downstairs, where I knew Ethan would be waiting. I searched for him in the kitchen and found him sitting across from Dad at the table. Locke was at the counter with a bowl of cereal, and Liam was pouring himself a cup of coffee.

"Bad night," I yawned. Ethan looked concerned. I found myself an empty, clean cup in the cupboard and poured myself a cup of coffee too.

"Too excited to sleep?" Locke teased, winking at Ethan. I blushed. I was making it too easy for my brothers.

"No," I protested a little too loudly. Ethan moved over a seat, and I took his chair, in front of Dad. Dad was having toasted frozen waffles doused in maple syrup. He had test papers piled next to him that he had been going through before his waffles materialized. There was a threatening red pen on top of the stack of sad papers.

"Who fed the father?" I asked. Dad grunted.

"Technically," Locke responded. "He took my breakfast." Locke pointed at the waffles with his spoon, dripping milk on the counter. "I made that for me, and he took it when my back was turned."

Dad feigned innocence. "I thought it was for me," he claimed. "It just happened to be waiting for me right when I walked into the kitchen. What a kind gesture for the hard-working patriarch of the family." He took another bite of the waffles and smiled at Locke.

From that display alone, one could surmise how the family atmosphere evolved. It was dictated by the self-proclaimed hard-working patriarch of the family. It was this sense of humor that was passed down to his children. Particularly to the men.

Locke snorted and waved an empty box of Eggos at me. "We're also out of waffles," he complained.

"Noted." I took a sip of my coffee. The bitter hot liquid was the official start of the morning. While I was a proponent of sweets and all things chocolate, I liked my coffee black. It was the perfect counterbalance. "And I'm guessing we're out of Frosted Flakes too." I eyed the box next to Locke.

Locke looked in it. "We will be. Shortly." He grinned at me.

"Did you have something to eat?" I asked Ethan. He lifted his cup of coffee at me. "Same as you," he said. I frowned. I was failing at my duties as a proper host. "Do you want a better breakfast? Maybe an omelet or something?"

"Where's my omelet?" Dad complained. I pointed at the waffles. "You already stole someone else's breakfast. You don't need to have two breakfasts."

"She'll be 'right," Ethan said. I learned that it was his way of saying "Don't worry about it."

"Low maintenance," Liam commented. "I approve." He lifted his own cup of equally proportioned coffee and cream to Ethan in salute.

"We obviously can't put off grocery shopping any more," I declared. "Up for shopping, Locke? Or still lacking beauty sleep?"

"Fueling up for the excursion as we speak," he said, not looking up from his phone.

"Last chance," I warned Ethan. "You may need more than just coffee to get you through grocery shopping for my family." He raised an eyebrow, but did not take me up on the offer. "Don't say I didn't warn you," I added ominously.

Expedition

"Do we really need *two* carts?" Ethan asked.

Locke was walking ahead of us, pushing his own. Three containers of baked goods had miraculously materialized in them in the amount of time it took me to get Ethan his cart.

"Because Locke," I said by way of explanation, pointing out the two jars of peanut butter Locke had added to his own quickly filling cart. One smooth and one crunchy.

"Amateur," Locke chided over his shoulder. "We've only just begun!"

A mom walked by us with a toddler trailing. An infant in a car seat was taking up most of the space in her cart. The toddler, holding tightly onto her fluffy mint green comfort blanket, bumped into Ethan and staggered a few steps. She looked accusingly at him as if it was his fault, paused for effect, then stomped dramatically around him after her mother.

I snickered. "Is it too late for that omelet?" Ethan asked in a flat voice. I added two loaves of bread to our cart, considered that, then added a third. We're going to be hosting Thanksgiving for seven people this year. I'd rather overcompensate.

"I did warn you," I reminded him. "Feeding your entire squad of disciplined soldiers is probably less stressful than feeding my brothers." I eyed the bag of donut holes that Locke added into his cart. Between him and Dad, that would last one sitting. "We're going to need to get actual food and not just the sugar that Locke is stocking up on."

Ethan paused. "Hold up. *You* are advocating *against* sugar? You?"

"I like my sugar concentrated," I replied haughtily. "There are standards. You can't just dilute it with sacks of flour." I tilted my chin up and tossed imaginary long hair into the wind. He laughed and continued to push the cart.

We let Locke wander into the snack aisle while we detoured to the meats and dairy. "We're going to need a few sticks of unsalted butter. I'll go get those. Can you grab a couple of gallons of milk?" I asked.

Ethan lifted the elbow of his slung hand. "I can probably grab *one* jug of milk," he said.

"Oh, right! Sorry!" I tiptoed to give him a kiss on the cheek in apology. "You're just so capable," I smiled. "Easy to forget."

In the next moment, he wrapped his free arm around me and pulled me close. "Oh, you have no idea," he whispered. Both the sensation of his lips so close to my ear and the slow manner in which he said it, sent a tingle through me.

Just as quickly, he let me go. Then he winked.

I thought I was attracted to the secretive, brooding Ethan that I had met in the *wop-wops* of my dreams before, but this happy, confident Ethan was a different level all together. It was still exciting to be near him, but it was also more comfortable. Less like I was picking out the red-colored Gobstoppers and more like I was enjoying all the changing colors.

I hadn't realized that I once was so careful when I was with him, afraid I'd say the wrong thing that would affect him negatively. The difference between who he used to be and who he is here was equally reflected on me. I'm different, too.

I liked me more now, too.

I pointed out the butter brand I wanted, and he went to collect them. I turned to the milk shelf, a smile still on my face.

He's magical. Mundane chores such as this are elevated to cherished memory just because we're together. He's like that extra layer of cheese on your lasagna. The bacon topping on your salad. He makes the unfavorable palatable and the good even better. He doesn't even have to be doing anything. I'm just happier knowing he's here. This is the everyday I want for myself.

I was about to open the clear refrigerator door that housed the milk when a cold hand grabbed my arm.

And just like that, I was sucked out of my happy place and thrown into that darkened alley with a pale, hairless figure. I forgot that I was still standing in the middle of *Trader Joe's* about to stock up with dairy. In my head, I was trapped in a vortex and terrified beyond measure. A sharp inhale was all I could do before fear paralyzed every action.

"London?" Ethan's familiar voice, just as abruptly, yanked me back. I blinked. An associate announced a special on avocados over the store's speaker. The lady that passed us at the entrance was now trying to comfort her crying infant while her toddler tugged at her sweater. A sign made with permanent ink was urging me to try the new Vanilla flavored Soy Milk. Nothing unusual.

My one hand was still on the handle of the refrigerator door. I looked down to the origin point of this sudden junket to the nightmare in my mind. Ethan's hand, still cold from fetching the butter, was holding on to my other arm. That sensation was what triggered my anxiety attack.

"Hey, are you 'right?" He spoke slowly but also with a slight urgent concern. I hadn't yet responded and I could see that if I delayed a little longer, he may resort to more drastic measures.

"Ethan," I exhaled. Just saying his name was an elixir of sorts. I looked up at him and could see his guarded relief.

"What happened?" he demanded.

I shook my head, partially in response and partially to clear it. "Just anxiety, I think? From the nightmare." He hadn't let go of my arm. He waited for a better explanation.

"I've been having freaky dreams the last couple of nights," I admitted.

"Like dreams where you visit some other bloke in a different country?" His inflection was relaxed but I could tell it was more in an effort to put me at ease. I smiled at his attempt.

"Like *nightmares.*"

The crease between his eyebrows deepened but he rubbed my arm gently, encouraging me to continue. I abandoned the milk temporarily so that I could face him, and this matter, more directly. "I'm always in, like, some foreboding dirty alley with an alien thing." His eyebrows shot up and his hand paused.

"Wee green men? Tentacles?" he prodded.

"No, but, like, pale and smooth. It dresses human though," I offered.

"What is it with you and aliens?" he asked. "Why is your first instinct to always go with aliens?"

"It's not *always* my first instinct," I claimed. But he was right. And it felt good to know that he knew me that well.

"So what did this pale, smooth alien want?" he asked. I shuddered involuntarily, remembering the haunted look in her eyes. He picked up on my reaction and serious concern replaced his teasing expression. I looked down at my untied Chucks, reminding myself that I was standing here with him and not in my nightmare.

"I don't know, actually." A college student sporting the local school sweater needed to reach the milk. Ethan and I moved a respectful distance away. The interruption helped me distance myself from what was going on in my head. "She didn't seem like she was in good shape," I continued. I bit my lip. "She said she needed help."

Ethan was taking this more seriously than I had expected. I hadn't really taken the time to process what I thought about this and having this conversation was helping me too. "Is it just a dream? Or are you …" he paused, searching for the right term. "… *Skipping*?"

"*Skipping*?"

Ethan shrugged. "What do you call it when you dream and end up somewhere else?"

I never thought about a term for what happened between us. "Magic?" I suggested.

He lifted an eyebrow and flattened his lips together. "Fine. Well then, was it just a dream or were you *magicking*?"

I laughed. "OK, yeah, that sounds lame."

"It was your suggestion, not mine," he reminded me. "I liked 'skip' but it wasn't good enough for you …"

"I don't know if I was *skipping* …" I started to say.

"See?" he cut me off, shaking his head. "Better than *magicking.* So dumb …" He grinned, baiting me. I stuck my tongue out at him but I smiled. I was feeling better already. *He* was magic.

"I don't know if I was *skipping,*" I repeated, "I mean, it felt just as real, I think. And I remember it just as clearly. But when I dreamt about you it was always something different. This is repetitive. Same scene. Same series of events …" I waved my hands helplessly about me, failing to find the right adjectives to describe the dream. "It's really the feeling that I can't shake, you know?"

At that exact moment, my phone buzzed in my back pocket. I jumped forward, actually stumbling into Ethan. He caught me and held me tightly to him. I felt the rumble in his chest when he chuckled.

"Like that feeling?"

I detangled myself and fished my phone out. It was a text.

Brieann: Ryd Tmrw? Army boy coming 2?

I frowned and replied with just a question mark. Ethan was looking at me with the same punctuation reflected on his face. I shrugged. "Brieann. I think something is going on tomorrow but I don't understand --" My phone rang. I almost dropped it.

"Yeah?" I knew without looking that it was Brieann, calling because she was too impatient to explain over text.

"Are you not coming to Drew's big unveiling thing?" I didn't answer right away. I was backtracking in my recent memory for a mere hint of what she might be referring to. She picked up on my hesitation. "*Caden's*? Mural? Art Society?" She supplied. I felt like I was in a bad game show where I was supposed to figure out the common link between a set of unrelated words.

"Wait," I said slowly, trying to make sense of what I knew and what she thought I knew. "Are you talking about the project he's been working on?"

Drew had been showing me iterations of sketches and paint pallets over the past few weeks. It was a huge assignment he had been stressing over. It made sense that it was over Thanksgiving because the theme of the assignment was gratitude or something to that effect.

"Obviously," she said sarcastically.

I was still very confused. "Why *Caden's*?"

There was a pause on her end. Then very slowly, like she was talking to a victim of a head injury, she responded, "Because. That's. Where. The. Mural. Is."

The light in my brain was dim and slow to burn. "Oh! It's a mural!" There was a very impatient sound coming from her side of this conversation.

"What did you think this was?" she asked in undisguised frustration.

"I thought it was, like, a final for one of his classes or something. I didn't think he meant it was going to be a public mural!" Drew was a talented artist and well deserving of the attention. Now, his artwork was going to be permanently displayed. At our favorite restaurant, no less.

"This is a big deal," I said aloud.

"Welcome to the party," Brieann said, "So glad you were able to catch up."

"How did I not know this?" I asked, confused at my own confusion. I looked at Ethan for help. Hearing just my side of this conversation, he had no idea what was going on. In fairness, even if he heard both sides, he probably still wouldn't know what was going on.

Then again, maybe he'd actually know more than I did.

Drew had been there when I really needed him. He sat by me and slowly helped me gather the pieces of myself so that I didn't get blown away with depression. I don't know if I would have been able to navigate the past few weeks without him. He had been my anchor. He was incredible.

I'd been so wrapped up in my own life that I took for granted that my friends had events going on in their lives too. As if my world was the only one that mattered. What did that say about me?

"I'm a bad friend!" I realized. I felt sick. Like chugging-an-entire-glass-of-spoiled-milk-in-the-back-of-a-hot-school-auditorium sick.

"Does that mean you're not coming?" She asked, sounding confused.

"Of course I'm coming!" I practically yelled into the phone.

"That's why I'm calling!" She yelled back. "Do. You. Need. A. Ride, Psycho?!"

"Yes! I need a ride!" I was still being loud but couldn't stop being loud. "Are you picking me up?!"

"Of course I'm picking you up!" She was even louder. Ethan wasn't just hearing my side of the conversation anymore. He was also taking a few steps away, distancing himself from the whole spectacle. It wasn't over yet.

"Good! What time?!"

"I don't know! 10?"

"Fine!"

"Fine!"

I hung up, then stared at my phone in silence. I looked up at Ethan. He was about six feet away from me at this point and watching me without looking at me. An older gentleman walked past between us. I saw Locke push his cart toward us. He glanced at Ethan first, then at me. I was still holding my phone limply in my hand, not saying anything.

"What's with all the yelling?" Locke finally asked.

I blinked at him. Locke looked at Ethan.

"From what I can suss out," Ethan said slowly. "Everything is all keen, yeah?"

Locke pursed his lips, blinked at Ethan a couple of times and then looked at me. "I don't know what that means." He then pushed past us and headed to the chips aisle. "Don't forget to pick up waffles," he called over his shoulder before he disappeared behind the stacks.

Homebase

When we were younger, Dad put my brothers in charge of unloading groceries while he and I sat in the kitchen and organized the pantry. He taught me to put the newest items in the back so that the older ones got used first. Every can had to face the right way and stacked just as they had been in the store. He always got at least two of the same items when we shopped. Some items, like fruit snacks, didn't often make it to the end of the day. Other items, like beans, stayed in the pantry until there was almost nothing else left to eat.

Grocery shopping was an expedition that we did once a month. In between the big trips we picked up perishables. Sometimes. Sometimes we went over a month without stocking up and had to rely on take out. Because it was just Dad and me in the house, we hadn't needed to do any large shopping trips. This was the first time in months that I've had to do this. The ceremony was oddly comforting.

I went through each bag methodologically and found a spot. Except for the bag of Jacked Doritos that Locke came into the kitchen eating while he carried the last of the groceries in.

"That's all she wrote," he announced between bites. It was his way of announcing that all the groceries had been brought in and his job was done. I waved him away.

"Good. Thanks. Get out of the kitchen." It was the response he had expected. He happily turned on his heel and walked out with his precious bag of chips.

"I think he does that intentionally," Liam observed. He leaned back at the dining table where his laptop sat open. "So that you won't find other things for him to do."

"He's served his purpose," I said. Dad was probably back at work, finding new and creative ways to torment poor college students over their Thanksgiving break.

"When is Chase getting in?" I asked, handing Ethan a couple of soup cans to put away.

Liam didn't look up from his laptop. "Hell if I know," he responded. "I think he's grabbing an Uber; so we may not even get to see him until Thursday."

I paused. "Why the cloak and dagger?"

"It's Chase," Liam said by way of explanation. "He probably wants to make a grand entrance or something."

"Yeah," I agreed. "Sounds like Chase. Well, I've got a thing tomorrow anyway. I mean, Ethan and I do."

Ethan and I.

It was a phrase that still sounded unfamiliar but had the echo of something long established. I liked it.

"Do you need a ride?" Liam offered out of habit. Ethan, grinning, put his finger on his lips to remind me not to shout. I stuck my tongue out at him.

"We're good," I responded within acceptable decibels. Then to Ethan, "Make yourself useful." I handed him more cans of soup and pointed to where they would go in the pantry.

"Just don't yell at me," he teased, ducking out of the way before I could shove him.

Pod People

Ethan and I were already waiting on the porch steps when Brieann's silver Volkswagen pulled up at five after ten the next morning. Ethan opened the front passenger door for me before he got into the back. I hadn't expected it, but I found that a part of me enjoyed the attention. Growing up in a family of roughhousing brothers, I've had to fend for myself. It was nice to be on the receiving end of gallantry.

Brieann's telling smile meant that she was enjoying the show. I rolled my eyes at her but I was smiling too.

"Good morning, Ethan," she said in a sing-song tone when he got buckled in.

"Good morning," he parroted back at her in the same tone. I looked at her questioningly. I was now very suspicious of the innocent smile.

She shifted into gear and pulled away from the curb. "The unveiling is in fifteen," she said, making a very wide right turn.

I couldn't remember the last time I was in her car, but the wide turn reminded me that I was sitting in the death seat. I knew I shouldn't criticize, particularly because I didn't drive, but sometimes, it was just hard to ignore.

Fortunately, the speed limit in town wasn't more than 35 mph, and in a car, took less than 10 minutes to get there. The threat to our lives wouldn't last long.

"There's going to be press there," she was saying. "This is going to be great for his chances at an art scholarship." She always had her finger on the pulse of what was happening in our little town. I was often a reluctant participant by her side but for once, I was grateful that her knowledge prevented me from missing this.

"Thanks for the ride."

She shrugged. "I know you'd normally take your bike but I figured that you couldn't tandem with Captain Kiwi." She turned on to the main road, five miles below the speed limit and narrowly missed a college kid on his bike. I cringed. She wasn't fazed. "It isn't really Tristan's scene anyway, and I didn't want to go alone."

Ah, the cardinal rule of high school … you're only as strong as the posse you ride with. Lone wolves don't survive long.

We found parking at a public lot a few stores down from *Caden's*, where we didn't have to attempt parallel parking. The diner's lot was partially blocked off with bright orange cones to make room for the event. A small crowd gathered. I recognized a couple of teachers and the school Student Affairs Coordinator. There was a photographer with three cameras around her neck walking around but not taking any photos. She seemed more concerned with the hors d'oeuvres than the schedule.

I finally spotted Drew as we walked closer. He was standing next to a wall, covered with a tarp. One could surmise that this was a special occasion because he wasn't dressed in his usual green flannel over a novelty shirt. He had not given up his beat-up Vans or his everyday jeans but he had on a crisp white button down shirt, an olive green jacket, and a bright yellow tie. He waved when he saw us.

"You guys made it!" he exclaimed, excitement on his face. Then he spread his arms wide. "How cool is this, huh? We're going to be a town landmark."

"It's just legalized graffiti, you sellout," I teased, greeting him with a hug. He stumbled back, pretending to have a knife in his heart. "The pain … Oh, I die, Horatio … the stab of jealousy quite o'ecrows my spirit …"

"An exhibit and a show! Double value!" I applauded, laughing.

He straightened up and took a bow, "Be sure to give me five stars in your review."

"Congratulations, Drew," Brieann said, ever gracefully.

Drew's smile for that greeting was much less mocking than the one I received. "Really glad you were able to make it," he responded genuinely.

Mr. Williams, advisor to the National Art Honor Society, put a hand on Drew's shoulder for his attention. "We're about to start," he warned, indicating that Drew had to join the rest of the team.

We stepped back and found a place with the crowd to watch the ceremony unfold. The photographer was starting to use one of her cameras; so things were about to get official. Drew's excitement was infectious in a really good way.

I held Ethan's hand and leaned against him. Here we were together doing harmless, non-perilous, teenage things. I was enjoying this on a much deeper level. Not everything had to be on the brink of danger for it to be significant.

Mr. Williams opened up with a background on the National Art Honor Society, introducing the team of eight artists that worked on this together. I didn't really know anyone else on the team.

Drew was the project captain and the last one to be introduced. He looked equal parts proud and embarrassed by the attention.

Mr. Williams then went on to explain the joint project among *Caden's*, the city, and the organization. He talked about how this was a meaningful event, particularly before Thanksgiving, where we reflect on what makes us grateful.

I looked up at Ethan. I had much to be grateful for this year.

When the tarp was finally pulled down, there was a flurry of applause and the photographer snapped away, cycling through her cameras. It was like a small town red carpet event. I clapped and cheered with the rest of the crowd. Drew now looked 80 percent embarrassed.

The mural was multimedia with bits of colored rock and mirror adhered to the brick in unison with the paint. It was a successful merging of eight different styles. Drew had spearheaded the project; so much of it was his vision. I could see his favored surrealistic style echoed throughout, even underlining the others' work. The signatures of all eight artists, located at the bottom right, completed the painting. The photographer was taking plenty of close up shots of it.

Brieann had her phone out and pulled us close to her so we could take a few selfies together. Why I hadn't thought of that on my own, I didn't know. Ethan had been here three days, leaving in four, and we haven't taken a single photo together. I pulled out my own phone to get in on the action.

Brieann, of course, recognized more people from school and was pulled away into the crowd. I continued to take more pictures of just Ethan and me. He looked awkward in the photos. I gave him a kiss on the cheek in one and that helped him relax a bit.

"I'm using these for future alleged sketches so you may want to smile better," I said. That made him laugh and I was able to catch that on my phone. It was better than any drawing I've made thus far.

Drew found us. "Hey, where's Bree?" he asked, looking around.

"Socializing," I responded. "Isn't that what you're supposed to be doing?"

He sat on the curb. "I've got people for that." He waved at the direction of his advisor.

"You mean you're hiding?"

He leaned back on his hands and grinned. "My vision is realized. My work here is done. Let the peons squabble amongst themselves."

Brieann was back. "London, can I borrow Ethan for a bit?" She asked me like he was nothing more than a pencil she needed for a test. Like he wasn't a person standing right there. Like he couldn't hear her. I looked back at her in disbelief but thankfully, Ethan wasn't at all offended. He had raised one eyebrow and a smile tugged at the very edges of his lips.

I looked down at Drew, wondering if I was the only one that found this behavior inappropriate. "It's the accent," he explained to me with sarcastic patience. "It means he doesn't understand English. Obviously. Maybe she needs you to translate."

At least it wasn't just me.

"That's not what I meant!" Brieann complained with impatience.

Drew gestured at Ethan. "Talk to him, not me!"

Brieann wrinkled her nose at him as if she had smelled something unpleasant but did what he suggested. "I just want to introduce you to some people," she said to Ethan. She was once again dignified and poised.

Unlike Locke, Ethan didn't generally like people. I tensed up. "Are you OK?" I asked him. I wasn't sure what he was expecting from this trip, but I had a feeling it wasn't this.

"She'll be 'right,'" he assured me. "This is all very educational." He grabbed my hand and brought it to his lips before he allowed himself to be led away.

I still felt the heat in my cheeks when I sat down next to Drew. Together we watched Brieann introduce Ethan to a small group of people. I recognized this enthusiasm. She did the same to me when we had first met. She absolutely loved this. Brieann Hendrixson, diplomat to the world.

"I wonder if he regrets being here yet." I said it in jest, but I did worry a little.

"I think there's a long scientific word for the kind of neurosis you have," Drew observed. It was his version of reassuring me. I hit him on his arm. It was my version of thanking him. "A long, violent scientific word," he amended, rubbing his upper arm. I hadn't hit him hard, but he liked to pretend I did.

"Just because you're a celebrity artist now, it doesn't mean you get a free pass," I warned. Reminded of his new status, he quickly shifted gears. He tossed his head in the air for the full hair-flowing-in-the-wind effect. It would have been more effective had he had longer hair. Or wind. As it was, his imaginary locks were enough for him to brush back unnecessarily. "Peasant," he said in mock disdain.

"Seriously though, well done," I said, changing the track of our conversation. The banter was fun but he deserved sincerity. He relaxed and leaned back on his hands again.

He looked up at the completed mural. From where we sat, we could see the wall in its entirety. There was a humble look of pride on his face.

"Thanks," he accepted. "It turned out better than I thought it would, actually. Beth's additions were a good idea." He was talking about the bits of colored glass. "I forgot how different it was to work with acrylics," he mused. "I had to adjust. Not a bad job."

"Not at all," I agreed. "Food is a forgiving muse."

The twinkle in his eye was my first indication that I had missed something. "Is that your takeaway here?"

"There's something more?" I teased. Drew was an artist through and through. There was always a reason for his work. He didn't create just because it was pretty. I can always count on his artwork to have a deeper meaning. But I didn't always know what it was.

He winced. "Ouch. You wound me."

"The press release isn't out yet on your artist statement; so you're going to have to explain your work to me the old-fashioned way."

"It's a mural of gratitude!" he exclaimed as if that was all that was necessary. That wasn't a revelation. That was the title. The mural was that of a traditional Thanksgiving feast. Entirely appropriate for the restaurant wall where it was painted.

"And you're grateful for food?" I nodded sagely but I knew that wasn't what he meant.

"Yes, food is always something to be grateful for," he admitted. "But it's also a metaphor."

I laughed. That sounded like Drew. "Of course it is. Like your Bologna Sandwich of Life Theory?"

He pointed at me with one hand and tapped his nose with the other. "See? You do know me," he insisted. He waved his hand in a general encompassing way to include the entire mural. "Each food group represents something to be grateful for in life."

I looked at the painting again, intentionally keeping what he said in mind. Art appreciation changes when you consider the artist's intent and not just the first impression you get from it. What was the message past the obvious? There were bountiful breads, vital water, and even decadent wine. They were metaphors to suggest different levels of blessings. From the most basic necessities to luxuries that we may take for granted.

The more I looked, the more I saw. The empty glasses still waiting to be filled could stand for the potential that drives us to succeed. The utensils that are tools to help us achieve our goals. The fruits of our labors. The threads on the diner cloth that weave us all together. The message was there. All with a mix of realistic and vibrant colors. The sun reflected on the bits of mirror, making it sparkle. It really was an impressive display. A fantastic symphony of visual art. And even more impressive, knowing the artist responsible for this.

"Nice realistic touch to include the stain on the cloth right there," I pointed out.

"Good eye!" He had a wan smile. "Every experience we go through contributes to who we are, right? Even the ones that aren't fun. They can leave a stain on your soul, sure. I know it feels weird to be grateful for those but without them, we wouldn't be our unique selves."

It was a revelation but before I could reflect deeper on that, his attitude changed. He pointed near the top of the mural, where a depiction of multicolored peas helped frame the painting. "You're in there, you know?"

I didn't see anything but peas. He was waiting for me to understand. I didn't.

"I'm a pea?"

He nodded enthusiastically. "Yep. You're definitely a pod person."

I wasn't sure how to take that. "Like a *Body Snatcher*?" I asked, confused.

He put both hands on his chest. "The fact that you know that reference just further proves my point." Before I could react, he continued. "But, no, not like the movie. Or the book. I mean like peas in a pod." He looked straight at me, his smile hovering between wistful and wonder. "Soulmates."

I shifted uncomfortably. I wasn't sure I liked where this conversation was headed. I could not have this discussion with him with Ethan just a few steps away. It felt disrespectful.

He picked up on my discomfort. He grinned to break the tension. "You know, soulmates don't have to be romantic."

"Don't they?"

"Not in my pod world," he replied with confidence. "I mean they can be," he clarified. "But they don't *have* to be." I believed him. I was listening. He continued to explain his Peapod Theory. "Peas that share a pod have a unique connection to each other. It's not the same with any other peas outside their pod." He made a little cocoon shell by putting one hand over the other. "They're soulmates either because they were exposed to the same environment that made them who they are, or they understand each other in a way that isn't dictated by time or circumstance."

He opened his cocoon hands up to my direction. "You understand this. You grew up in the same place all your life. But you come here and leave everyone behind without a second thought. They were friends but not soulmates. Possible peas but not of the same pod." I wanted to argue. I couldn't. He made sense. I did feel exactly that way. I didn't interrupt.

"You and I, though. We're of the same pod. You're one of my pod people." He leaned forward, resting his arms on his knees and looking up at the mural. "I'm always grateful to meet my pod people."

I considered what he said and marveled at how secure he was with his reasoning. There was merit in it. I had never felt connected to anyone before moving here. In the short months here, I've found rooted relationships that were undeniably significant.

We looked toward an opening where both Ethan and Brieann were walking back to us. I could almost see them both as round, green vegetables. I smiled at the visual in my head. "Some peas are more surprising than others," Drew observed.

Indeed.

American Holidays

"What's *Friendsgiving*?" Ethan asked me. We decided to take the long walk back home from *Caden's* instead of hitching a ride. Brieann still wanted to stay. Drew had to stay. I wanted to get back in case Chase stopped by. I didn't mind walking, and I certainly didn't mind walking with Ethan. I might have worried about his comfort. But the New Zealand Defence Force had a more rigorous training curriculum than a leisurely walk through town. This was barely a blip on his radar.

"Well, there's Thanksgiving, right?" I was fully aware that Thanksgiving was an American holiday and wasn't going to assume that everyone in the world knew what it was.

He nodded. "The invasion of indigenous people, right?" he asked sarcastically.

I took the bait. "Oh no, no. That's Columbus Day. I'm talking about Thanksgiving, where colonists were saved from starvation by said indigenous people."

He nodded again, looking very serious. "Oh, I see … I see," he concurred, rubbing his chin in mock thoughtfulness. I bumped him with my hip. He rewarded me with that half smile of his.

"Thanksgiving is always on a Thursday. You spend that time with family. Friendsgiving happens on Friday, the next day. You spend that time with friends."

Walking down the street with Ethan reminded me of walking with him through the boondocks he called the *wop-wops* when we first met. Except this was the suburban version. Instead of hopping over a stream, we were walking around drains and watching for traffic. "Usually, you bring a bunch of Thanksgiving leftovers to share with everyone. Sometimes a bunch of people go Black Friday Christmas shopping together." I shrugged. "It's really a free-for-all."

It was Brieann's idea, of course, to have a Friendsgiving get-together at her place. It might be easy enough to guess who she would invite, but when it came to her, there really was no telling. This could be an intimate affair or half the class might be there. It could go either way.

A month ago, I might have cringed at having another social obligation. Things were different now. This sounded like a lot of fun.

I glanced sideways at Ethan. He was the new constant in my equation that changed the value of everything.

"Are you OK with me dragging you around everywhere?" I asked as I stepped up on a higher curb and balanced on the edge. He was still taller.

"Seeing London in her natural environment?" His accent took a different pitch. More Aussie, less Kiwi. He brought his hand up to his eyes like he was looking through binoculars. "Crikey! It's dangerous but also so exciting!" I made a goofy face. "I'm learning a lot about you," he added, putting his hand down and reaching for mine.

I held his hand.

"Like what?"

"I'm not prepared to divulge that information just yet," he said elusively, slightly swinging my hand forward as we walked. "I've only just begun."

My mood had been lighthearted but then, without much warning, I felt a weight. I just remembered that we've burned through the days like a fast camera shutter, and we were running out of time. A week had been a blessing. Now the days felt like a somber countdown. It was a mix of emotions that left my stomach turning and a sour taste in my mouth. It was disturbing how the internal struggle can affect me on such a physical level.

He picked up on the change immediately. "Yikes," he tugged at my hand. "Does someone need more sugar?" He reached into his pocket and pulled out a couple of fun-sized Snickers. He offered one. "Open slather at the art event," he explained. "You know ... just in case."

Oh, he really was learning a lot about me.

I accepted the offering of chocolate, and my mood shifted just as quickly. I smiled. Better already.

Meeting Lincoln

Locke threw the door open just as we reached it.

"Thought you were Chase," he said when we walked past him. He took another look behind us before closing the door.

"You're like a hipster waiting on the new iPhone," I said, both mildly amused and mildly annoyed. I kicked the pile of size 12 men's sneakers that migrated their way near the front door. Perfectly positioned to trip me.

I had forgotten what it was like living with brothers.

"More like a toddler waiting for the ice cream truck," Liam corrected. He was sitting on one of the two wingback chairs in our living room, his laptop on the side table next to him. "Chase said he was picking up lunch on the way over." That explained all of Locke's eager anticipation.

"Where's Dad?" I asked.

Liam pointed with his stylus. "He kicked me out of the guest room. Said he needed an hour or so to finish grading a few papers. The kitchen table wasn't doing it for him." I looked down the hallway to the kitchen and could already see the dishes on the table that had not been put away.

"Gee," I said sarcastically. "I wonder why."

Locke hadn't stopped looking out the front window. "I bet the wingnut stopped at his hotel first," he complained, still obsessing over Chase. A low growl from his stomach was perfectly on cue for maximum effect.

I exchanged a look with Ethan and rolled my eyes. *Oh, the drama.* "He probably should've anyway," I said. "It's never fun bringing luggage around."

Locke didn't look away from the window while he spoke. "He's here for three days. What luggage?"

Liam also didn't look away from his screen when he responded. "You know there's a full luggage and a carry-on involved. It is Chase." They were having an entire conversation without once making eye contact with anyone in the room.

I walked away, and Ethan followed.

"Not in your room!" Locke yelled. How nice that he took the time out of his hungry self pity to humiliate me that way.

"I think Chase is here!" I yelled back, winking at Ethan. I heard the front door open. Followed by Locke's frustrated moan.

"Not funny!" He yelled.

Chase arrived an hour later. Locke had already had two bowls of cereal and found a stash of microwavable corn dogs in the freezer. I don't even remember buying corn dogs, but he had eaten them all before we could send them out for carbon dating.

I was the one that answered the door.

A tall dark-skinned man, who was decidedly not my brother, was the first person I saw. "Hi," he said, flashing his straight white teeth at me. I didn't respond right away. His smile faltered a little and he looked uncertainly to his left. He was sharing a look with someone but I wasn't interested in who. I was more interested in this new person standing in front of me. So much so that I didn't even see Chase until he handed me the bag of fast food he was holding.

"This is for Locke," Chase said. "And, hello to you too, London."

I accepted the bag automatically even before I turned to really look at him. I hadn't seen Chase in almost a year. A lot can happen in a year. His hair was a little longer, curling around his ears. He was wearing dark rimmed glasses in place of the wired ones I had last seen him in. He looked good.

"Chase!" I said unnecessarily, reaching up and throwing my arms around his shoulders. He answered my hug with one of his own.

By the time I let go, I had collected myself. I looked back at the new guy, who was looking a little less uncomfortable but still uncertain. "Hi," I responded to his earlier greeting. "I'm London." I reached out a hand to him.

"This is Philip," Chase said, by way of introduction. The way he said *Philip* was significant. There was an almost indistinguishable change in tone. His voice deepened a fraction. It meant something. I looked sideways at Chase. He was watching my reaction. Watching for a reaction.

Philip took my outstretched hand. "Nice to finally meet you, London," he said politely. "Lincoln has told me a lot about you."

I raised an eyebrow. "That sounds dangerous. Don't believe any of it. Unless it's awesome ... that's legit." It was cordial banter but Chase didn't relax. "Come on in." I stepped back. "Meet the family," I added, sharing a look with Chase as they both walked by me.

"Dad!" I yelled as I closed the door. "Chase and his date are here!"

Locke had left the kitchen for the promise of more food in the form of the take out bag I was holding. Liam had abandoned whatever he was working on. Philip had their attention. There was a heavy silence in the air.

After a beat, Locke shrugged. "Yeah, that explains a lot," he said, taking the bag from me. "Good meeting you, man," he said to Philip. Philip responded with a small wave. The uncertain smile still frozen on his face. "Thanks for the grub, bro," he said to Chase, lifting the bag in salute. Then he walked back into the kitchen.

That was significantly less painful than Ethan's introduction to him.

Liam shook Philip's hand, but didn't say anything past greetings. He was waiting on Dad.

Chase and Philip looked so uncomfortable. I could relate on some level. It was akin to how I felt when I introduced Ethan to the family.

"Ethan," I said into the silence. My voice sounded like an echo even when there was none. "This is my brother, Chase. And this is Philip." Chase looked startled, like it was the first time he registered that someone he didn't recognize was standing in the room. It may very well have been the case. He looked at me, then at Ethan, then back at me, putting together the pieces of the unsaid puzzle. Very much how Liam was looking at them.

Possibly because he was in a very similar situation, Chase's reaction was friendlier than our siblings' had been. "Oh, sweet," he said, about to extend a hand before he noted the sling. He dropped his hand and inclined his head in greeting instead. "I didn't know my sister was bringing someone to dinner, too."

"I didn't know either," I mumbled to Ethan's amusement. Before I could elaborate, Dad walked in the room. He was looking down at some papers in his hand.

"Did you have a good flight, son?" he asked, without raising his head. Liam cleared his throat. Dad finally looked up and stopped mid stride.

"Hey, Dad." Chase said. There was a slight nervous tremor in his voice. He put one hand around Philip's shoulders and introduced him. "This is Philip. My boyfriend." Philip extended his hand. Dad took it automatically but the blank look on his face meant that the motion was more reflexive than anything else.

Dad blinked a couple of times without saying anything. He was processing the information. Chase's lips flattened into a tense line. The seconds stretched longer than it should have. Each measure of silence was another painful twist for Chase. I felt for him. He didn't have the support of the Secret Service like I did when I introduced Ethan to Dad.

"How long have you guys been together?" I asked, when I couldn't take the discomfort any longer. I didn't know if it was going to make things better or worse, but I figured having it move one direction or another was better than the limbo where we seemed to hover.

They first looked at each other but before Chase said anything, Philip responded with a smile. He didn't look away from Chase. "I met Lincoln at *Wizard World* last August ..."

Wizard World might have been the least surprising bit about this. I glanced at Ethan and he looked thoroughly confused.

"Wondering what *Wizard World* is?" I asked teasingly. "He's from New Zealand," I offered to Chase and Philip as an explanation.

"Actually, I'm wondering who Lincoln is," Ethan said.

That made me laugh. Liam grinned and even Dad smiled a little. Locke walked back in the room, a mouthful of double cheeseburger, as if summoned by the good humor. Although confusing Ethan even more, It broke the tension.

"Lincoln is actually Chase's real name," I said. It had been a while since I've had to explain that. It was fun falling into the familiar dialogue. I knew my response didn't answer any questions. I still enjoyed seeing the mounting confusion.

"Our dad basically raised us all to prefer BMWs over any other car," Locke explained. "But when the Transformers movie came out, Chase …"

"You mean Lincoln," I interjected gamely.

"Sorry, Lincoln," he amended. "Lincoln became obsessed with the Camaro …"

"Bumblebee." This time, Chase himself made the correction. Locke ignored him.

"The CHEVY Camaro," I supplied helpfully.

"Bumblebee," Chase said again. Everyone ignored him. Philip put a hand on his shoulder in consolation.

"I tried," Dad added. "The hardtop convertibles … the z3s … the Ms … nothing worked."

"In fairness," Liam said for Chase's sake. "None of those turned into robots."

"The hardtop convertibles transformed," Dad asserted. Liam shook his head. It was an established argument.

"I'm still confused," Ethan admitted. He would have probably been more sarcastic if it were anyone but my family he was speaking to. "So why … Chase?"

This time, everyone laughed a little. Well, everyone but Chase. Chase was looking upwards. Possibly for strength to get through this conversation. Philip was grinning.

"Well, it's a Chevy Camaro," I said again, more slowly. Ethan looked at me blankly.

"Chevy … Chase?" I asked as if it were obvious. Ethan shook his head, still at a loss.

"He's an actor," Liam supplied. "Before your time," he said to Ethan.

"Or not your side of the world," Locke suggested. He crumbled up the empty cheeseburger wrapper.

"He's not that old, and he's known all around the world," Dad argued defensively. There was collective eye-rolling but no one corrected him.

"Chevy Chase is an older American comedian," I explained better. "So instead of calling him Chevy, we just called him Chase." I shrugged. "It stuck. I've known him as Chase since before I was in the double digits."

"Is it Lincoln now?" Locke asked Chase. He was mocking him in a way that only a brother could.

Chase sighed. "You do realize that technically, it was *always* Lincoln, right?"

"Semantics," Locke dismissed him.

"I don't really care either way. The fifth generation Camaro is still a bitchin' set of wheels." Chase adjusted his glasses. "I'd call it an American Classic, even."

"It can't be considered a Classic if it's less than 20 years old," Liam pointed out.

"Semantics," Chase said in the exact same way Locke had.

Dad pointed his papers at Philip. "You!" The sharpness of his delivery cut through the discussion. He put Philip on the spot. "Chevy or Bimmer?"

The entire room held a collective breath.

Philip first looked at Chase, almost in apology, before answering. "German Engineering all day, every day." He tilted his head to the side in a half shrug. "It's the ultimate driving machine."

Someone did his homework. There was approval in the form of a collective exhale.

"Well," Dad said in resignation, throwing his hands up in the air. "Chase may not know how to pick cars but at least he can pick a guy that does."

Favorite

Dad and Liam were sitting at the table with both Philip and Ethan. Locke was leaning against the counter, strategically positioned to be both interested and uninterested in the conversation.

Chase and I were standing together on the other side of the room, watching the suburban kitchen interrogation act unfold like a cheesy holiday movie. He had a dark beer in one hand. I was eating a Twix bar.

"You've had a busy few months," he said, tilting his drink toward the mild pageantry.

I snorted. "This is one of those pot-calling-the-kettle moments, right?" His lips twitched. I smiled.

There was a pause where neither of us said anything. It wasn't the first stretch of silence since he and Philip arrived, but it didn't make it any easier. Every one of them was clumsy. The air was heavy with so many unasked questions but I didn't know how to begin asking them. It made me uncomfortable. I cleared my throat. He didn't offer any assistance.

"This was gutsy," I said, almost casually. It didn't fool him. It was forced, and he could tell. The next sentence was not nearly as casual but it was the best I could do. It was too late to back down. "Bringing the boyfriend home for Thanksgiving." He didn't answer. He chewed his bottom lip and nodded absentmindedly.

We watched the scene in silence with a sense of removed attachment for a few minutes. Then I started watching him.

There was a noticeable crease of worry between his eyebrows that hadn't gone away since I opened the front door. His muscles were tense. He barely drank his beer no matter how many times he put it to his lips.

"How long have you known?" I asked him abruptly. Subtlety wasn't working. He turned to look at me, his expression lacking surprise. He was expecting this question although still seemed slightly unprepared. He put the bottle to his lips again. He didn't drink.

"I think I've always known," he said but it sounded like a question. "Or maybe I never really cared for labels."

"You had a girlfriend, though," I said, confused by this big reveal. I never thought of myself as woke but I thought that I knew enough. I was quickly learning that I didn't know anything past the popular propaganda.

"I did," he admitted. "She was my best friend; so I thought that's how it was supposed to be, you know? And when it didn't work out, I thought it was because we just didn't work out as a couple. That happens too. It was all very … expected." He stared down at his bottle, but it wasn't really what he was seeing. "There wasn't really anyone that I was particularly attracted to anyway; so it didn't really matter either way."

He looked at Philip and there was a ghost of a happy memory reflected in his expression. "Then I met Philip and stuff sort of just made so much sense."

"I can't believe you didn't say anything," I complained. "I know I'm not on your speed dial. But I can't believe you didn't tell me before bringing him to meet Dad! You couldn't send a text?" I was only semi-acting like I was hurt. Part of me was genuinely offended at being left out of the loop.

"I'm not worried about you," he snorted, rolling his eyes.

"You're worried about Dad?" I asked, surprised.

"Bringing someone home is one thing. Bringing *him* is completely different." The happy peace on his face melted into uncertainty. "Does Dad even really know anyone who isn't straight? How does he feel about one of his sons being … queer?" He looked down at his beer, moving the liquid around in little circles. His vulnerability was painful.

He was six years older than me but, at that moment, he looked like a child.

Chase was always the most private of my brothers. It was an expected byproduct of his inherent geek personality. He kept to himself and his interests. It was just how he was, and no one thought anything of it.

He always seemed to be the sibling most sure of himself without apology. The one never afraid to be different. He was tea when everyone was coffee. Kale when everyone was having bacon. He was the one who would never succumb to peer pressure.

It didn't occur to me to consider that his steadfast sense of self was an indication of any kind of internal struggle.

I didn't answer right away. His exhale was heavy with the weight of doubt.

I couldn't tell him how Dad was feeling because I had no idea. Ethan had made everything that I thought was predictable, unknown. The world was now a surprising place to be. I couldn't comfort Chase with any sense of confidence. I could only tell him how I felt.

"I think," I said, carefully measuring my words, "that it's more concerning that you felt that you had to hide anything from us at all."

His bottle stopped spinning but he continued to stare at it. There was no way to tell what he was thinking. My heart hurt for him.

Meeting Ethan had made me feel both significant and isolated at the same time. I thought I was losing my mind. It was a defining moment in my life, and I didn't feel like I could share it with anyone honestly. It was the kind of contradiction that causes internal logic to fail and systems to break down. The stress of it literally made me sick.

How did Chase feel?

I took his silence as an invitation to continue. "I think," I said again, still carefully, "I would have loved to know that you met someone as dorky as you." How would it have been if Chase actually told us? If he texted the group chat to say that someone in cosplay asked him out? How would that conversation have played out?

"I would have loved to hear about your first date. I would have loved to share the anticipation and maybe … no, *definitely*, I would want to contribute to the anxiety." He smiled at that but continued to stare at the unmoving bottle.

In my case, had I just been honest with Dad in the first place, he would have been able to tell me that I wasn't crazy. That Ethan was real. That my feelings were legitimate.

"I don't care that you're gay or bi or queer or if you turned out to be a *Klingon*. I just care that you should know that you can always, *always* talk to me."

When he finally looked up, there was a shine in his eyes that wasn't there before.

"Thanks," he said. He put an arm around me and hugged me close. I could smell the sweet malt of his dark beer in his hand. It was never as appealing to me as it was at that moment, made sweeter by the comfort of knowing that everything was going to be fine. He kissed me on the top of my head. "You're my favorite sister."

I laughed. "Actually, you may be my favorite brother." He pulled away to look at me with both eyebrows raised and his hipster glasses sliding off his nose. "Your *favorite* brother? For real?"

I pointed at Philip. "Until you showed up, I was in the hot seat. Now, Ethan is old news and you're making headlines. Thanks for giving them a new target." I laughed at my own joke and Chase pushed me away.

"Forget you," he said. "Locke is my new favorite sister."

Ch–ch–ch–changes

T minus 72 hours. Or so.

It was Thanksgiving.

Meeting Philip was unexpected but it also gave me a perspective on how the rest of my family was dealing with my relationship with Ethan.

Poor Dad, I thought. I knew that raising four kids by himself was probably not easy, And now he was getting hit with a lot of new material these past few months. I was impressed by how he pivoted in place, all things considered. First with Ethan, and also with Philip.

Despite all of Chase's apprehensions, everything turned out fine. He finally lost the crease between his eyebrows and allowed the good natured ribbing that accompanied all of Philip's stories. We contributed to the vault of embarrassment with stories of our own. The house hosted more laughter last night than it had heard since we moved in.

By the end of the evening, Philip was also calling him Chase.

Dad shook Philip's hand again before they left and he gave Chase a long hug. I couldn't tell who benefited from that more. They both needed that. They had said something to each other but that was between them.

I had laid my head on Ethan's shoulder as I watched this all unfold. My whole family together again and a house full of love. My heart was full.

It was the perfect way to end the night.

By morning, all I could think was that in three days, Ethan would be leaving.

Per tradition, Dad had gone out earlier in the morning to pick up the annual Thanksgiving breakfast box. It was the main source of nourishment for the family up until Thanksgiving dinner was formally in play. This year, he visited a local bakery. There was an assortment of bagels, croissants, muffins, and donuts. There were also six turkey shaped cookies in a separate box.

"One for each of you turkeys," he said when he unboxed it on the dining table.

In that one action, he demonstrated how much he accepted both Ethan and Philip.

"Save it until after the main meal," I admonished Locke when he went straight for it.

"But it's part of the breakfast box!" he whined.

"It was in a *separate* box," I argued, if he was going to get technical. "I want Chase and Philip to see the full set before you behead one."

He grumbled something but contented himself with a cherry-filled breakfast bomb instead.

Ethan wasn't much use in the kitchen with one hand. It wasn't for lack of desire to help but, in practice, it made more sense that he stayed out of the kitchen during prep.

Locke was definitely not welcome in the kitchen.

The two of them banished, Locke took Ethan under his wing and made it his mission to teach him the subtleties of American football. Ethan didn't look enthusiastic but it was OK, Locke was enthusiastic enough for both of them.

It fell to Liam, by default, to slice and dice while I baked, threw ingredients in pots, and stirred sauces. They were familiar assignments and we fell into our roles comfortably. It had been years since we started this together, and we've since become adept at our tasks.

"No experimental dishes this year, I see," Liam observed. He thumbed through the hardcover sketchbook I had used to write down recipes, in no particular order, that I intend to duplicate. Some pages have been stained with actual ingredients from repeated use. Others have been forgotten. Desserts were written at the back of the book for "easy" access. Multi- colored post-its marked the ones for special occasions. Like Thanksgiving.

We had been in the kitchen almost two hours straight hopping between the pasta, mashed potatoes, casseroles, and chops. The dishes all cooked simultaneously but with staggered start times in hope that they all finish in perfect crescendo.

"I think there are enough random elements involved this year. We don't need to push all of Dad's limits." I sprinkled the casserole with grated Parmesan cheese while I talked. Cheese always made everything better.

"Some things are just so different, you know?" I added, opening the oven door to reach for the dinner rolls.

A high-pitched piercing tone almost made me drop the hot pan. The smoke alarm had gone off. Liam threw his palms instinctively over his ears. I had both hands occupied so all I could do was squint, as if the action had any influence on my hearing. Locke came charging in, Swiffer in hand, like a modern knight-in-a-worn-out-pullover-and-sweatpants. He pushed the handle up to the offending machine, aiming for the small pause button.

It wasn't the crescendo that I was hoping for.

Finally successful on his fifth try, Locke leaned back on the counter with exaggerated relief. He eyed the rolls on the pan I was still holding, then plucked one out before I could react.

"Payment for services rendered," he claimed, bowing out of the kitchen, hot roll in one hand and modern lance in the other.

"And yet," Liam observed after his exit, "some things never change."

Traditions

We had to extend the dinner table to accommodate everyone. The close quarters contributed to the Norman Rockwell atmosphere of family tradition. Except that in a glance, we didn't look like anyone's idea of a traditional family. Missing a mother. A gay son and his partner. A weird daughter and her dream boyfriend.

"I thought American Thanksgivings meant turkey," Ethan observed.

And we didn't do turkey.

"You would think," Locke acknowledged as he loaded his plate with an unhealthy amount of carbs. He passed the veggie plate to Philip without taking any for himself. Instead, he doubled his helping of bacon mac and cheese. "Our family doesn't do turkey."

There was a family resemblance in all the smiles that my brothers and I shared at Ethan's confusion. Philip looked like he'd been warned ahead of time.

"Their mother hated turkey," Dad explained. He cut into his chicken, swirling it into the gravy he had put on the side. "She always had turkey for Thanksgiving growing up, and it didn't bother her, one way or the other. The year Liam was born, we decided that our little family will be celebrating Thanksgiving on our own. It was the first …"

"… and last …" Locke interrupted. Dad pointed his fork at him in agreement.

"Yes," he admitted. "And last time that she attempted."

"Too much work?" Philip asked.

Dad laughed. "Let's just say the turkey didn't turn out quite the way she was expecting."

"Burnt on the outside, bleeding on the inside," all his children said in near unison. We laughed. It was a tradition in itself that Dad repeated this story every year. Dad grinned, nodding at the chorus.

"We had takeout that year," he added.

"She wasn't into cooking much?" Philip nodded in understanding. "My mom hates having to do all the cooking so we always visited relatives for Thanksgiving."

Dad shook his head. "On the contrary, she was an excellent cook. She never really did follow recipes very well. Other than the turkey, the end result was always good. "

"And never repeated," Liam added.

Dad shrugged. "She never wrote anything down; so every dish she tried to repeat was always changed one way or another." He nodded at me. "You must've inherited that gene. Similar method, similar results."

I didn't know if it was the off-handed compliment on my cooking skills or the way he compared me to my Mom that I liked best. Sometimes, I felt like they just ate what I made because they didn't have much of a choice. Hearing the affirmation spoken aloud did wonders for my self-esteem and pride. I couldn't even fake modesty. I smiled, basking in the glow of honest appreciation.

"So much like your mother," Dad said. It was a phrase that, when uttered in frustration, was probably the reason I had been able to get away with so many things growing up. It was undoubtedly the reason I was the favored child. His expression had softened into a bittersweet mix of loss and comfort.

Everything I needed to learn about love, I learned from my parents.

"I'd do pork chops over turkey any day and twice on Thanksgiving," Locke declared. As if to prove his point, he pushed his dinner roll off his plate to make room for a second chop.

"You did a great job," Ethan said to me. "The grub is brilliant." He had sampled a little of everything on his plate.

"Yeah," Liam agreed. "Worth having to deal with the smoke alarms going off every year."

"It doesn't go off *every* year," I argued over the laughter. "It didn't go off *last* year," I pointed out as an example.

"You took down all the alarms last year," Locke accused. "And literally tossed them out in the snow!"

"*Buried* in the snow," Liam emphasized.

"You killed them," Locke continued. His voice had grown

louder just so he could talk over the laughter around the table. "We had to dry them out in rice!"

"Yeah," I admitted without regret. "But they never went off."

"The only person I know that waterboarded a smoke alarm into submission," Chase mumbled to Philip, loud enough for everyone to hear. I narrowed my eyes at him. "It's a skill," he assured me, winking. I stuck my tongue out.

The laughter subdued into a conversation casserole of sorts. Everyone talked at the same time but not necessarily about the same subject. Voices fell into a comfortable level of noise. They overlapped without drowning anyone out. It was a flow that was in time with the sound of flatware on plates or drinks being poured. Food seemed to be in constant motion around the table. There would be a spike of laughter or jeers but always falling back into a natural volume.

The scene framed by the glow of the kitchen light made me stop. It was something that had never happened before. Not just because Ethan and Philip were a part of the picture but because it was the first of traditions to come. Thanksgiving at our new house. With all my family.

It was almost enough to help me forget that, in three days, Ethan was leaving.

Almost.

Countdown

Long distance was where relationships go to die.

Thanksgiving dinner was over. The dishwasher was near the end of its second load. The few leftovers we had were properly labeled and stored. The only items left on the table were a few dessert plates, the dessert, and Locke. Dad was already asleep on the couch. Liam's laptop was operating in the living room where Chase and Philip sat, watching the Thanksgiving rerun of *Friends*.

Ethan and I were sitting on the porch steps together. He had his legs stretched out in front of him and he was leaning one elbow back on the step behind him. A picture of one content and completely relaxed. It was a good look on him. I should have joined him in that moment and shared that happiness but my insides were in knots. The more perfect the moment, the more dread I felt.

I needed more time. There was still so much we needed to catch up on. So much we needed to learn and do together. We needed to establish something more concrete to hold on to before taking it into that challenging level. I pulled my hoodie around me, trying to warm the cold that wasn't caused by the weather.

"Are you … crying?" Ethan asked, suddenly tense and alert.

The guilt for ruining the picture of his contentment was the tipping point. "No," I lied, even as I felt fresh tears quietly making an unattractive path down my face. I looked away so I could wipe them off.

"What's wrong?" The alarm in his voice was intentionally tempered.

I shook my head. I wasn't trying to be dramatic, but I was also worried that if I tried talking right away, I would start wailing. I knew he was here with me right at that moment. I knew that this was to be celebrated. I knew that it made no sense to feel this awful when everything was just so good. The heaviness of his future absence was overpowering, crushing the fragility of this moment. He pulled me into a hug. The warmth of his embrace was another reminder of what I'll be missing, and I started crying into his shoulder.

He held me patiently while I tried to get the words out. "I don't want you to go," I said slowly between breaths. He squeezed.

"Oh, London." He didn't let go of me. He held me so tightly that whenever I moved, I ended up wiping my face on his shirt.

"I just wish we had a little more time," I whined.

He pulled away from me and held me at an arm's length. I kept my head down, embarrassed by irrational emotion. He lifted my chin so that I'd meet his eyes. Contrary to my display of woe, his lips were pulled in a half smile and the green in his eyes twinkled.

"About that," he began. There was something in his voice that made me stop mid-sob. He touched my face, attempting to clear the tears that I had hastily wiped away. "I was waiting on my CO's approval before I said anything," he continued.

I held my breath. This was going to be followed with big news, and I wasn't sure if I was going to like it or not.

"And I talked it over with your father." He took both my hands in his one. "I'm extending my leave. I get to stay for another two weeks."

Two weeks!

I threw myself at him and he almost fell back. "Ow, ow, ow!' he protested. "The arm!" I eased off a little but didn't let go.

Two weeks!

Suddenly, the heaviness on my heart was gone and I was swallowed back up in that feeling. That feeling of gratitude and infinite possibilities. Two weeks wasn't forever but it stretched out longer than the hours I had been counting down. Two weeks more of him. Two weeks more of us.

Another round of tears exploded, but this time, accompanied by laughter. I wasn't prepared for the dual emotions and struggled to balance myself. When I finally pulled back, the laughter had won over the tears. He was favoring his shoulder but looking at me with some measure of pride for a mission accomplished.

"Are we still crying?" he asked, confused. I was crying for completely different reasons.

"I'm happy," I assured him, but it was still between breaths. It was hard enough to talk when you were laughing. I had added crying to that mess. It wasn't my most distinguished moment.

"My strange, strange London," he said affectionately, pulling me close so that I could hide in his hug.

Best. Thanksgiving. Ever.

Nightmares

I stepped into a puddle.

My Chucks were not made for moisture. The disgusting sensation of dampness leaked into my thin socks. I lifted my foot out of the wet patch and shook it. It was an attempt to drain my shoe. Instead, it sloshed the liquid around more evenly *inside* my shoe and also splattered a little outside on my jeans.

So smart. Not.

I shoved my hands in my hoodie pockets and side-stepped the puddle. At least my left foot remained dry. Once on dry, well, drier, ground, I looked around.

In a moment my eyes adjusted to the little light. My stomach sank. It wasn't so cold this time around. The wind had calmed but the unease remained. It was a modification to the last time I went through this. I wouldn't necessarily call it an improvement. I would probably take the cold over the wet.

My dentist said there was evidence that I was grinding my teeth while I slept. She said it was usually caused by stress or anxiety. It was a bad habit that would lead to headaches and other dental issues down the road. Dad had bought me a night guard. I wore it for all of one month before it found a more permanent place in my nightstand. I didn't even bother packing it when we moved.

Maybe bad dreams caused stress and anxiety. I made a conscious effort to unclench my jaw. Let's avoid that plastic jail mold if we can.

The uneven, discolored city lights created unnatural shadows. A low fog concealed the landscape. The only element missing was a slow, broken vaudeville soundtrack. Unfortunately for me, it played in my head anyway.

As expected, she was there waiting for me.

The dull colors of her shawl almost blended into the tinged night. Above the fog, silhouettes and sharp lines were all in focus. Except for her. Was it because I didn't really want to look? I knew that I had to, at least to progress through this nightmare and get it all over with. I've unintentionally belted myself into a carnival ride of unstable consequences.

She barely moved. Everything about her confirmed that I was dreaming. She seemed spectral, a phantom-like manifestation of an unspoken fear.

As if my presence triggered a hidden remote, she looked up. The gears of the dream continued to crank, and I found myself walking unbidden toward her. Her eyes alternated between sharp focus and lost in a different time. She saw me and saw through me. Just like I did her.

"Help ... Please."

Her voice was low and broken. A glimpse into the shattered soul that spoke the words. Her emotions were powerful, creating a forceful energy that felt like a wall. Or a silent, deafening scream. I didn't know what to do. Her eyes shifted focus again and her expression was that of desperate loss and hope. She existed in a constant state of contradiction.

"How?" I asked. I was helpless and very much afraid.

"It's so cold," she whimpered, pulling at her shawl. The fog danced around her like magical smoke. I took my hands out of my pockets. The air was still.

She shivered when there was no chill, and she pulled her shawl completely off regardless of her perception. The lights emphasized her bald head. Shadows shifted with every movement. She made a rough bundle in her arms, pawing and wrapping. Shaking the entire time.

"My baby … my baby … please …"

Save for her shawl, her arms were empty. I strained to look through the fog. I looked behind her and, hesitantly, turned around. We were completely alone.

If you can get hurt in a dream, you can probably die in one too, I reminded myself. I ached to help but I was terrified. I was alone in a dark alley with a crazy woman. I did not know how dangerous she could be.

I was grinding my teeth again.

She found me, her hallowed eyes capturing mine in a desperate grip. "My baby," she said again. "She's going to die."

It began to rain.

Solid Ground

The elation of sleep, fresh from the news that Ethan would be staying longer, was forgotten when I awoke. I was drenched with discouragement not unlike my Chucks had been.

Except my Chucks were perfectly dry, tossed over a pair of dirty jeans where I had abandoned them beside my door. Outside, the sky was clear. No evidence of rain.

The nightmare had left emotional and psychological marks, not physical ones.

I pulled my sheet over my head, but that reminded me too much of how the figure had worn her shawl that I immediately pulled it off. I kept my eyes open, paying attention to everything around me, grounding myself to the present.

Earlier in the summer, I had painted my room in colors that reminded me of Ethan's eyes. He had just been a fantasy at the time, but the connection between us had felt so strong and I wanted it to continue. I had wanted something real to represent what I had thought was too good to ever be true.

I had never been able to regulate my dreams before, and this was no different. At least when it came to control.

Having this recur made it feel familiar. The immersion was familiar. The intensity was familiar. But unlike dreaming about Ethan, this was not something I wanted to experience, much less repeatedly.

If I believed that dreaming about Ethan was destiny, what did that mean about this nightmare?

The morning was forgiving. I had fallen back asleep some time between four in the morning and waking up. The aftertaste of the bitter nightmare had faded, and the sun helped me shove the experience to the back of my mind. I didn't want to waste my limited daytime thinking about monsters of the night. Especially not when I had better dreams to appreciate. I found myself able to smile before I got myself out of bed. The temporary roommates were already seated at the kitchen table, chatting over Liam's laptop and some coffee. Both of them looked up at me when I entered the room. Ethan stood.

"Anyone hungry?" I asked, more out of habit than any real offer to make anything.

"You're kidding, right?" Liam responded, lifting his mug. "I need help digesting yesterday. I may not have room for the next week." Ethan agreed. His mug was empty.

I took that as a compliment.

"Bree is having a Friendsgiving thing later today; so Ethan and I won't be home for dinner," I reminded him as I helped myself to some of that coffee they were both enjoying.

"There are enough leftovers to cover us. And if Locke polishes it off, there's always pizza," he responded, unconcerned. "I don't think he'll be waking up before noon; so that's at least one meal we won't have to feed him."

"What does one wear to a Friendsgiving?" Ethan asked.

"A kilt, I think," I suggested teasingly. "It's a very formal affair."

"I need to do laundry then," he replied gamely. "I wore that on the plane, and it can get pretty dodgy."

"Lucky for you we have this thing called a washing machine. Do you need help operating it?"

"Cheers." He left the room, presumably to collect his laundry. I sat down on his vacated seat across from Liam.

"I hear the boyfriend is staying longer," he said with too much nonchalance to be nonchalant. He didn't make eye contact. I recognized this approach. Dad had sent him in to gather intel.

"I'm the last to know, apparently." We were playing a game. The object of the game wasn't entirely clear to me yet but for whatever reason, I felt like I was the one with the advantage. It was a good feeling. It made me hungry.

The plate on the table still had a small selection of baked goods from Dad's Thanksgiving morning run. I picked up a chocolate croissant to go with my coffee.

"Arrangements had to be made," he said, still not looking at me. Whatever was on his laptop screen was evidently too riveting for him to look away. Yet, not demanding enough to skirt this conversation. "It was a good move on his part to come to us first."

Ethan may have been able to balance his approval rating despite his bold request. He was navigating these uncharted waters better than I.

"I'm glad he did," I agreed, attempting to get on the right track that Ethan had blazed before me. I took a bite of the croissant. "How did Dad react?"

Liam finally looked at me. "Are you happy?" he asked, not answering my question.

I met his gaze without blinking. I swallowed but waited a beat to answer just so he could see that my response was both thought through and sincere. "I'm very happy," I said slowly, further emphasizing the earnestness I hoped to convey. "He makes me very happy."

Liam searched my eyes, trying to see if there was something I wasn't telling him. I had nothing to hide. I took another bite and smiled. He must have known that I was honest, but he seemed reluctant to believe it.

"I know this past year hasn't been easy," he began. "I just want to make sure that you aren't using this," he gestured toward the doorway that Ethan had exited from. "You aren't using *him*," he amended. "As an unhealthy coping mechanism."

I didn't know what I was expecting. Maybe a stumbling, embarrassing conversation that involved threats about being overly physical. Maybe a flexing demonstration of his authority as the big brother. I didn't think he'd delve into psychological behavior theory.

I sat back in my chair, seriously considering what he was saying instead of being offended by it. It was a tough year. There were so many changes that threw us all for a loop as a family. It was entirely possible that I was investing so much into this because it helped me channel my anxiety. Just last week, I had been questioning my sanity. Hadn't I described my relationship to Ethan in just those terms at least once before? Unhealthy.

"I guess I wouldn't know," I admitted, somewhat deflated by my lack of conviction.

Interestingly enough, it seemed to be what Liam was looking for.

"Good," he said.

"Good?" This didn't sound good at all.

"Yes," he confirmed. "Good." He shut his laptop. He no longer needed it as a prop for his feigned disinterest. He focused his full attention on me. I suddenly felt I had lost all that advantage I thought I had. He was always the better at strategy games and, more unfairly, I didn't even know the rules to this one.

"We can't always be certain where we stand, London," he said, sounding so much like a younger version of Dad. "But it's important that we at least check to see how stable it is before we start dancing."

Laundry

"You knackered?" Ethan asked. He was loading the washing machine while I was staring past him at a wall, busy contemplating my brother's words.

"Huh? Oh, yeah," I said, pulling myself out of it. "Restless night, I guess." It was an easier excuse to use.

He paused midway to throwing in a pair of soiled socks. "Good restless or bad restless?"

I shrugged. "I had that weird dream again." I wasn't sure I wanted to really talk about it. Talking about it gave it some kind of substance that I didn't want. As if ignoring it meant it couldn't possibly exist.

"Exactly the same?"

I picked up an almost empty jug of liquid detergent, swishing the liquid around and staring at the label so I didn't have to look at him. It reminded me of the liquid I dreamt was sloshing around in my shoes. I put down the jug.

I took my time answering as if the delay would make him lose interest. Maybe I was hoping that the answer would present itself without me having to think about it. He waited.

"No," I admitted, having to confront the question when I couldn't find the answer I needed on the detergent label. "I mean there were things that were exactly the same." The same alley. The same hairless figure. The same tattered shawl. The same sinking feeling. "But circumstances change, you know?" As if he would know.

He didn't pretend that he did. He threw the socks in. His eyebrows may as well have been a straight line over eyes that seemed to have darkened in thought. "Are you in danger?" That was always his first concern.

My instinct was to ease his worries, but he wouldn't appreciate the insincerity. He'd prefer honesty over false assurance. I pushed the detergent toward him. He looked at it but didn't pick it up. He waited again.

"I don't know. Nothing has happened so far. It feels like it but it could also just be plain old nightmare anxiety." I shrugged. "I don't even know for sure if I'm … *skipping*."

He smiled. "We fancy *skipping*, do we?"

I stuck my tongue out at him. "For lack of a better verb."

"You're a lack of a better verb," he said, laughing.

"That doesn't even make any sense!"

He laughed harder. "You don't make sense."

I picked up one of his dirty shirts and hit him with it. He avoided my flailing and collected me with his one free arm, pulling me close to stop my attempts. I dropped the shirt when his face was close to mine.

"You don't make any sense at all," he whispered. "But I love you anyway."

Unicorns

Ethan didn't have a kilt after all. Fortunately, a freshly laundered shirt with clean jeans worked just as well. The light knit top I had on wasn't the exact same color as his shirt, but I was pleasantly surprised to see that it was similar enough to match. I liked that we didn't plan it to be that way but it happened anyway. I didn't need more magic to believe that Ethan and I were meant to be together. But that didn't mean I wasn't going to enjoy it.

Ethan was unfamiliar with Friendsgiving but I've attended a few before. We've always had to bring a dish to contribute to the Smörgåsbord of food to be shared. It was a casual gathering of friends sharing leftovers.

Brieann did things differently.

At par with the rest of her parties, this had all the trimmings of a catered event. Instead of leftover turkey and ham on a slab, there were little turkey and ham tea sandwiches. All perfectly arranged in little towers and trays. Instead of casseroles, there were mini quiches. A variety of harvest themed desserts were accessible next to the punch. Festive music was playing throughout the house at a surprisingly low level. On point with the mood. She even had paper chains hanging from the ceiling.

What takes an entire committee and three months to pull off in school, this powerhouse of a party organizer gets it done in two days by herself. Well, herself and the willing volunteers that she recruits.

We arrived at Brieann's place over an hour before the party was to start. Not to volunteer. Volunteers were there much earlier. Brieann has long since accepted that I wasn't a resource she could tap for this, and we've moved on. I am happy to be one of the consumers of such efforts. That has also been accepted.

Nor was it because I was excited to be at this party. Or any party, really. I've attended many parties growing up as Locke's sister. It wasn't until Locke left for college that I realized that I didn't actually like being at parties. I liked to arrive earlier because then it looked like I was there long, and that meant I could also leave early without Brieann giving me a hard time.

Drew was the only other person there. He was one of Bree's resources that she recruited. Everyone else had either left to return fashionably late or were arriving late intentionally from the start.

"Sucker," I greeted him.

He was putting together yet another paper chain to add to the mob. The remains of a sandwich were pushed to the side. The chewing motions suggested that we just caught the finale of said sandwich. "She offered me food and this was better than lugging Christmas decorations from the garage, which is what my mother would have assigned me to do had I stayed home."

"Lesser of evils?"

He nodded. "At least this I can do sitting down."

"Where's Bree?"

"Who knows? Bedazzling the unicorns? Dress rehearsals with the mermaids? Something to make this party *trés incroyable*." He made air quotes with his fingers over the last two words. "That's French, you know?" he said to Ethan. "It means obnoxious and elitist."

Ethan grinned. "I reckon I've heard that before." He made a show of looking around before taking a seat next to Drew. "So this is another American tradition, is it?"

Drew snorted. "You would think," he said, before I could answer. "But there's really very little tradition about Brieann." He sealed the last paper ring and tossed it to the ground. "This is more like giving tradition a makeover on daytime TV and having it sashay down the overly lit walkway amidst admiring applause."

"Speaking of sashaying down the walkway," I interrupted. Brieann made her entrance. Her hair cascaded down her shoulders, carefully curled and party ready.

"You're here!" she squealed into my ear while she hugged me. "How great is this, right? Our very first friendsgiving together! It's going to be *trés incroyable*!" Behind her, Drew rolled his eyes.

This would be a standard Bree greeting, but there was something off about her over enthusiasm. I searched her face and could see that beneath the carefully applied makeup, the look in her eyes didn't echo her own words.

"It's so great," I agreed. "Hey, Ethan, can you give Drew a hand here for a minute. Bree wants to show me something."

"And a hand is about all he can offer," Drew said, pointing to Ethan's sling.

"I can arm wrestle," Ethan suggested good-naturedly but he was looking at me, reading between what I was saying. He may not have understood but he trusted me and didn't protest.

"While arm wrestling is super helpful for party prep, I think I'll pass," Drew played along. "You'd probably win anyway. Here, hold this tape down …"

I grabbed Brieann's hand and pulled her out of the room.

When we were safely out of ear shot, I let go and turned to face her. "OK, what's wrong?"

That was all it took. She started to cry.

"Tristan and I got into another fight," she said between sobs. She and Tristan were always fighting. This wasn't exactly new. The drama would have been tiresome and maybe even funny had she not been genuinely upset.

"What happened?" I asked, already regretting this conversation.

She slumped against the wall, staring at her freshly manicured nails, refusing to look at me. "We were on a video call this morning, like usual, right? I asked him to come by. You know, to help with the party and stuff." I nodded. A silent encouragement to continue. "He said he'd stop by if I gave him a little more incentive." She raised her eyes to me, telling me all I needed to know about the incentive that Tristan was hinting.

I didn't bother to hide my reaction. "Gross."

She looked back down, hiding behind a curtain of blonde curls. "Honestly, that's totally Tristan. Usually, I just ignore it but, yeah, I basically reacted the same way you did." Now, *that* was surprising. "Like, he shouldn't have to have *incentive* to want to spend time with me, right? Being with me should be enough *incentive*." Her voice was dripping with unveiled sarcasm.

I agreed wholeheartedly but I also knew this game. I'd say something derogatory about Tristan, she'd pile on it, it would escalate, we'd both be very angry at him. Then two hours later, they're homecoming king and queen again. I'm the only one angry. I'm the one who "doesn't understand".

Against my basic instinct, I offered him the benefit of the doubt. "Maybe he was just kidding." I was not very convincing.

"You'd think," she said. "But, nope. He was serious. He wasn't going to come see me otherwise. He even said he'd, like, boycott my party or something."

"So he opened with offensive bartering and then escalated to social extortion," I summed up.

"Pretty much." She sighed. "Then the name-calling started."

"Classy."

"Then before I could hang up, he ended the call!" Her outrage might have been more that he had executed that maneuver before she did than any actual feelings of rejection. She slid down the wall and sat on the floor. I joined her but didn't say anything.

When she spoke again, her voice was small and vulnerable. "I'm just so sick of it. The whole thing. I mean, at no point did I ever think I'd live happily ever after with Tristan, you know?"

That's a relief, I thought, but still didn't say anything.

"He's just a boyfriend," she mused. "He does all the boyfriend things. We do stuff together. He pays for lunch. He carries my junk. He doesn't go around cheating on me or anything." Despite listing Tristan's sterling qualities, she leaned her head back on the wall in tired resignation.

"We talk everyday but don't really talk. I have to repeat myself because he doesn't listen. Honestly, I don't even care what he's thinking, half the time." The emotional rollercoaster was starting to gain momentum. And volume. "I can't even remember the last time we laughed together. Like, for real, laughed together.

Sometimes, I don't even like him. He can be irritating. Just immature." She threw her hands up in the air then just as quickly, crossed them tightly in front of her chest. "Seriously, why are we even a couple?"

I pressed my lips together so that I wouldn't say anything I would regret. This was her trip and whether she decided to give it another go or get off the ride, it had to be her choice.

"I see how you and Ethan are together," she said. She lost the volume. Her voice was even and steady.

Wait. How did this become about me?

"There's, like, this intensity between you. It connects you even when you aren't in the same room." She looked back at the other room where we had left Ethan and Drew. "Sometimes it's easier being away from Tristan. I don't ever really miss him." She made a face mimicking distaste.

"You and Ethan … you actually *like* being together," she continued. "Even when you aren't touching, it's like you're still holding hands or something. All you have to do is look at each other and there's all this transfer of information and feelings and stuff." She closed her eyes. "I want that."

"You deserve that," I finally said. She opened her eyes, but they were filled with doubt. Not because she didn't think she deserved it but probably because she didn't think it existed for her.

"High school isn't about who you date," I said with a confidence that I didn't realize I had. "I always figured that I'm too busy trying to figure out who I am and what I want. I wasn't ready to do the whole dating life."

"Says the girl with the perfect boyfriend," she interrupted, but she was smiling. I smiled too.

"I don't know what I'm doing, to be honest," I admitted, my

sudden bout of confidence had disappeared as quickly as it came. "I'm still trying to figure out what it is to be a good friend."

"I think you're an excellent friend," she assured me. She stood up, her ego healed and armor back in place. "Tristan and I aren't excellent friends. We're barely friends anymore." There was decision in her tone and that, more than anything, fueled her. "I'm done playing this game with him. I'm done letting him ruin my day."

She flipped her curls away from her face. "Friendsgiving is about friends. Not gross ex's."

Friendsgiving

"Are you having fun?" I asked for possibly the twenty second time in as many minutes. Miraculously, Ethan wasn't as annoyed as I would have been had our roles been reversed.

We were at a high school party. Albeit it's been *Brieann-fied* but still technically a high school party. It was one of those regular events couples did together. But being that this was our first one, much like our first date, that meant this was sort of a couple's milestone.

Ethan put down the red solo cup and took my hand. "Ask me again," he said, pulling me close to him. I smiled, tilting my chin up to him. The physical contact was calming and stimulating at the same time. It was a definite improvement over my high-level anxiety.

"Are you having fun?" I asked again, but my inflection had changed. I was more shy than I was anxious.

He leaned in to me so that our lips were just almost touching and I could feel the warmth of his breath.

"I ..." He kissed me.

"Am ..."

Kiss.

"Having ..."

Kiss.

"A ..."

Kiss.

"Great ..."

Kiss.

"Time ..."

Kiss.

Before he finished the sentence I was already laughing, and he was trying not to kiss me on my teeth. I hugged him and he laid his chin on my head.

"You're a hard case," he said with affection. I didn't really know what that meant but the way he said it made me squeeze him a little harder. He smelled of laundry detergent and California air. We swayed a little with the music. It was as close as either one of us would get to actual dancing.

Someone had cranked up the volume. To have a conversation, you'd have to be a notch below yelling. I think it was designed so that people would have to be in each other's personal space for any successful communication. It would have bothered me but the loud music created a byproduct of privacy that I was never in a position to appreciate before.

The party was two hours in, and Tristan wasn't there. His boycott attempt didn't seem to make any difference to the attendance, though. He and his testosterone crew, Sam and E, might have been absent but everyone else was still there.

I had to volley more attention than was comfortable as people had started to show up. I had missed significant school earlier in the month when I had my last seizure. Also the same time that I thought Ethan had died.

Rumors of why the new girl wasn't in school ranged from me having had a psychological breakdown to kidnapping. Kids I've never spoken to before actually hugged me when they saw me, acting as if they were invested in my well-being.

And, of course, everyone wanted to meet Ethan. It didn't escape my attention that there was a disproportionate amount of girls over guys that went out of their way to say hello. It might have been funny at first but the whole thing got old pretty fast.

"Americans are so friendly," Ethan teased me.

I rolled my eyes. "Especially the female variety, huh?"

"Did you hear that?" He lifted his chin sharply and looked around. His brows tightened together. I strained to hear anything out of the ordinary but the blend of voices and music hadn't changed.

"What is it?" I asked, slightly alarmed.

He grinned. "Sounded like jealousy."

I was not amused. He had picked up my family's brand of humor way too easily.

"You know, you're cute when you're jealous." He laughed at my expression but took my hand and kissed it. "You have nothing to worry about," he assured me. I wasn't convinced and refused to look at him. I allowed him to turn my chin to face him, but I was still looking to the side. Out of principle.

"As if anyone can compare." His voice was honey. Sweet and useful in soothing burns. Even the sting to one's pride. "I looked for you in waking dreams and found you halfway around the world," he reminded me.

That deserved eye contact. The magic in his hazel eyes reminded me that we had a connection unlike any other. Just as this wasn't a typical high school party, we weren't a typical high school couple.

"If it takes me the rest of my life to prove to you what that means to me," he continued. "So be it."

I forgave him even before our lips touched.

Crashed

"I think we can probably head out now," I said, glancing at my phone. "Your stalker fan club might miss you but I think Bree will be OK."

"Always leave them wanting for more?" He grinned at me.

We were weaving through the crowd to find Brieann when Tristan, flanked by his friends, walked through the open front door. I stopped walking so abruptly that Ethan walked into me. He was apologizing, but I was too busy frantically scanning the room to react.

Tristan found Brieann before I did. She was standing by the open patio doors, laughing with friends. He was closer to her than we were. I had started to push my way to her but Ethan and I were still on the other side of the room when Tristan got to her.

He grabbed her by the arm, making her spill her drink a little. Unafraid, she jerked it away from him and started to tell him off. He wasn't backing down either. The people around them fell away, giving them a tense center stage in which to publicly argue. I hadn't realized that I also stopped moving, like I had been compelled to stay in place and watch. Ethan stood next to me.

I don't remember if anyone had actually stopped the music. I just remember that it was completely quiet. It was the only way I could hear what was being said across the room.

Tristan's hands were balled into tight fists. Brieann had tears in her eyes but the way they were narrowed meant that she wasn't allowing herself to be a victim. This was an ugly, ugly fight. I started to push forward again. I didn't know what I was going to do, but I felt that Brieann needed someone to stand by her through this. The crowd was slow to move. They became obstacles that prevented our progress.

What they were yelling at each other wasn't nearly as important as when Drew, emerging from the crowd, put a gentle hand on Brieann and urged her to step back. Then he stood between them.

I hadn't realized until that moment how much muscle Drew actually had. I'd never seen him stand so tall and solid. His stance was concrete. It suggested that he was an immovable object.

"Go home, Tristan," he said in a very level, very quiet voice. It was devoid of the playfulness that was always present in every conversation I've ever had with him. The disparity made the little hairs behind my neck prickle.

"Or what?" Tristan challenged, but his tone was lacking foundation.

I felt Ethan tense next to me. A sidelong glance at him confirmed that he was assessing and was possibly already mentally in motion. The set in his jaw meant that his arm in a sling was of little consequence. I laid a gentle hand on his arm. He glanced quickly at me in silent acknowledgment.

These sheltered high school boys had no idea what kind of damage Ethan could do.

Drew didn't flinch. If anything, he was even more rooted in the spot. He didn't answer. He didn't have to say anything.

Tristan swore at him, inches away from his face. Drew closed his eyes against the spit from Tristan's words but he didn't move. Tristan pushed him once; then turned away before Drew completed the step backward.

The music started again.

Rain and Tears

Summer is my favorite time of the year. But given the choice between snow or rain, I'd pick snow every single time. You can play in the snow. You can make snow angels, build a fort, or sled down a hill. You can throw snowballs at friends, paint with food coloring, or snowboard. There was an entire Olympics dedicated to winter sports. Unending possibilities.

The rain just gets you wet.

This was a nightmare; so it wasn't summer and it wasn't snowing. This nightmare found that perfect combination of freezing rain. The worst of both conditions. At night. Of course it was night.

And because this was a nightmare, I was also ill prepared. Fortunately, not naked, but my hoodie wasn't sufficient protection against the elements. I was soaked through and shivering before I even took a step.

The rain was disrupting my vision but I knew there was shelter between the backs of the buildings. I knew exactly where I was without also not knowing where I was.

I knew she'd be there, hiding in the shadows. I hesitated. What was expected of me here? What was the right thing to do?

What won't get me killed?

As monsters go, she wasn't the worst. She was more like a misunderstood psychiatric patient than a demon looking to feast on my soul.

Like I knew anything about monsters. Horror stories were just not my thing. I knew the elementals: a wooden stake through a vampire and a silver bullet through a werewolf. She was neither and even if she was, it's not like I had a wooden stake or silver bullet.

Monsters are basic. Everything is about motivation. Monsters need to eat and we're just prey. They're motivated by hunger. Ghosts are different. They needed to do that whole unfinished-business-need-to-crossover thing. She was asking for help; so maybe she was a ghost.

How does one deal with ghosts?

I was also lacking a proton pack.

Maybe she wasn't a ghost. Maybe she was a different form of manipulative spirit monster that wants to suck out my happiness and insides by luring me with sob stories into her web trap of tortured souls.

Still lacking a proton pack.

I swore. It was a form of mental resignation.

Despite the appearance that I had multitudes of choices available, I still felt like I had few options. This scene had to play out. Standing out in the freezing rain wasn't doing anything other than increasing my chances of catching pneumonia.

Get sick here. Get sick in real life.

I'm a passenger in my own head.

She was where I was expecting she'd be, huddled in the corner of the tight shelter unintentionally created by the spacing of the buildings. Like a trick of the light, she was made mostly of shadows. I blinked to try and focus on her but she was elusive, like part of her shifted without even moving.

Once out of the rain, I removed my hoodie to wring it out. The cold made my skin prickle.

She didn't seem as agitated this time. She didn't even react to my presence. Instead, she was facing the rain, her shawl obscuring most of her features. She was a crumpled form of despondency.

I maintained as much distance between us as possible without having to step back into the rain. Maybe we can be like two ordinary strangers at a bus stop waiting for a ride, not necessarily having to interact with each other.

No such luck. She waited a few minutes before she turned her head, not directly to me but in my direction.

"It's so cold." Her voice was a sad whisper. She rocked slowly. I didn't respond.

She lifted her chin to look at me but her eyes were unfocused. I wasn't certain she was even seeing me. "My baby … my baby … She can't."

She pulled off her shawl. I was distracted by her smooth head though I expected it. When I looked back at her face, she was looking directly at me. Her eyes were no longer unfocused, but so sharp that the brown seemed like the only color in a black and white picture. In this black and white nightmare of a picture.

She was holding out her shawl at me. "Come here," she commanded. "I won't let you die."

Despite her assurances, my fight or flight instinct kicked in. The flight instinct was much stronger.

I stepped back, forgetting that I was standing against another building. My heels bounced on loose rock and the back of my head hit the solid wall. I spread my hands out behind me for balance, scraping the rough concrete. There was nowhere to go.

She took another step toward me.

I turned my head away and closed my eyes as tight as possible, as if that would make the nightmare go away.

I woke up.

Swirling Wheels of Energy

The party ended pretty much after Tristan's exit. Brieann was visibly upset; so I took it upon myself to kick out everyone. I don't think it was my intimidating presence that made them listen, but maybe having Ethan on one side and Drew on the other helped.

That also meant that it was up to just me, Drew, and one-handed Ethan to clean up what we could while making sure that Brieann was OK. We barely made a dent and we ended up staying out a lot later than I planned. Dad had already called me. I explained the circumstance and he cut me some slack. But not before he sent Locke with the X5 because he felt that it was too late to be walking home.

By the time Locke came to get us, we had moved the majority of the mess into the kitchen, but the decorations that had looked so fresh and festive earlier today were limp reminders of how the party ended.

We left Drew and Brieann sitting on the couch in front of the blackened TV screen. She had stopped crying and was just leaning on his shoulder. I knew from experience that Drew was an excellent listener. Brieann was in good hands.

The next morning, we met her and Drew at *Caden's* for breakfast. Although Dad insisted that the family spend the day together because my brothers were all leaving, he did agree it was my responsibility, as a friend, to check on Brieann. That gave me a free pass until lunchtime to be Brieann's Pod Person. I didn't know how long Drew and Brieann had been waiting for us, but Drew had polished off a short stack of pancakes before we even sat down to order.

Brieann recovered well. There was no evidence that she had been crying the night before. The slight slump of her shoulders and her smile not reaching her eyes were the only signs anything was bothering her at all.

And the extra tight hug she gave me as a greeting.

"Better?" I asked, grabbing the seat next to her.

"Yeah, I guess." She sat back down, picked up her spoon, and poked half-heartedly at the fruit and yogurt bowl in front of her. "My phone has been blowing up, and people are talking, but it is what it is."

"He's a douche," Drew said dismissively. "Making a scene like that at your party was a low blow."

It was a sentiment we had all expressed more than once the night before. But it felt like it needed to be repeated. I nodded along.

"Have you spoken with Amanda or Raven?" I was not their biggest fan but I understood they were Brieann's crowd long before I was a part of it. That meant something.

"Yeah. So. Much. Fun." She rolled her eyes. "Meeting them at the strip after lunch." She pointed her spoon at me. "You know, I had so much more patience for this crap before I met you."

I laughed. "Don't blame me. It was your idea to be my friend."

"You come with perks." She put down her spoon and sat back on her chair, crossing her arms in front of her. "Like maybe you can dream me up a better boyfriend." She was only partially kidding.

"You wouldn't want what I'm dreaming about these days," I warned.

"Are you actually dreaming up 'stached creepers with windowless vans?" Drew grinned at the inside joke.

"Scarier," I promised.

"Oh, I know!" Drew exclaimed. "Nothing is quite as frightening as a dream where you're peeing yourself."

We all laughed at that universal observation. Everyone knew that if you were dreaming up waterworks of any kind, that translated to a warm, wet mattress. You didn't even need special powers to make it happen.

"That I'd be able to handle." I shook my head as if that would shake away the conjured images. "No, these are more like horror movie nightmares. Shadows and hauntings."

"That's unsettling." Drew's grin was gone and he shared a look with Ethan in that heavy pause. "Does that mean those things will come true too?"

"Like, Final Destination style?" Brieann asked with wide-eyed concern.

I wanted to laugh it off, but the idea made me shift in my chair. "No one is dying or anything!"

"What do you see?" Brieann's voice dropped an octave lower

and took on a foreboding tone. She leaned forward on the table, her yogurt completely forgotten.

I looked to Ethan for support before answering. His expression was guarded but his eyes were a deeper shade of green with very little gold to lighten it. He was worried.

"I'm always in some dirty, abandoned-like alley. Sometimes it's raining; sometimes it's dry. But it's always cold and always dark." I closed my eyes to see if I can remember details better that way, and not be distracted by their reactions. "There's always this weird … being there." I avoided saying *alien*. Instead, I tried to focus on physical descriptions. I didn't want to think about the harrowed look she had or the emotions that it elicited.

"I think she's a she. She seems very effeminate anyway." I opened my eyes. "She's completely hairless. Totally bald … she doesn't even have eyebrows."

"So like a bald Mona Lisa?" It was Drew's way to lighten the mood. I smiled a little just so he knew that I appreciated it.

"She's covered in this big fabric wrap of some kind. Half the time, it's like she's so out of it. Like she's whacked out or drugged and doesn't realize I'm there. Desperate vibe."

"What does she want?" Brieann asked in the same low voice.

I thought about the fragments I've been able to make sense of. There wasn't much I could be certain of. "Help? I think? I mean, she says something about a baby. She's asking for help for her baby, maybe?"

Brieann put a hand over her mouth. This sounded too much like some Hollywood Horror.

"Well, that's ghastly." Drew declared. He was holding his fork halfway to his mouth. "That's like that urban legend of the dead hitchhiker. You give them a ride and they take your soul."

"That's not comforting," I shivered.

"No, it's not," he agreed. It wasn't meant to be.

"There's a lot of wailing and there's been some screaming; so there hasn't been a big exchange of information." I looked back at Ethan, considering how my experience had been with him. "It's different from when I dreamt about you," I said to him. "These nightmares are intense, but they're also shorter. With you, I remember spending hours visiting." I put air quotes around the word *visiting*. Ethan smiled.

"You mean when you were *dream skipping*?" Ethan suggested.

"Oh, is that what we're calling it?" Brieann asked.

Here we go again.

"Unless you can come up with something better. I've been failing," I admitted. When no one offered any suggestions, I pressed on. "And with Ethan, it's always daytime."

"That's not entirely true," Ethan interrupted. "You showed up on the roof in the middle of the night that one time."

I looked down at the scar on my arm. It had been my first real evidence that he existed outside my mind. He was right. We had laid on the roof and stared up at the stars. "Oh, right."

"So what does that mean?" Brieann asked, confused.

"It means Nightmare on London Street is probably in the same time zone as here." Drew was casual in his delivery but he looked bothered by the idea. I didn't like the thought much either.

"Tall buildings though, so it's nowhere around here, at least." I leaned back on my chair. "It feels real and all … just like with Ethan. But she doesn't look real. Like, she's out of place or something. That's why it's so hard to tell if I'm really … *skipping*." I was still having a hard time with that term. "It's like in between a regular, forgettable nonsense dream and …" I looked at Ethan. He smiled at me.

"You're both so gross," Drew said. Brieann didn't seem to agree with him. Her elbows rested on the table, her chin on her hands, and her head tilted to the side. Her smile was a mix of love-sick happiness and encouragement. Drew looked at her for validation, found none, and just shook his head.

"It's like you have a super-power," Brieann said from her perched hands. There was wonder in her voice. A much better tone than earlier.

"Like a mutant," Drew added with a grin. I stuck my tongue out at him.

"Where can I find my own personal *Professor X*, who can teach me how to control my powers?" I leaned against Ethan. "I'd love to be able to visit you whenever."

"We talked about this," Ethan reminded me again. "The last time you tried controlling this, you ended up in the hospital. I'd rather get an email than have that happen again."

"Maybe it doesn't have to be that serious," Brieann suggested. "She didn't always end up in the hospital when she was *dream skipping*." She said the term so casually, which gave it a strange legitimacy. I had a bad feeling that it was going to stick. "Maybe all you need is to unblock your *chakra*."

"My who-now?"

"Your *chakra*!"

At the very least, this topic was distracting Brieann. Tristan had left her to carry that soggy feeling of yuck. It was very unlike her to be so weighed down by it. I hadn't realized how unhappy it was also making me until I felt relief seeing her brighten. That alone was enough to entertain this conversation.

"Your *chakra* are points in your body that hold your *prana*," she tried to explain.

"Now you're just making up words," I accused. She laughed. It was her melodic signature and further evidence that this was healthy for her.

"It's a real thing," she promised. "Prana means energy."

"And why didn't you just *say* energy then?" I asked.

"Because saying made-up words makes her sound sophisticated and worldly," Drew teased. She turned her back to him and flicked her hair. It was a sophisticated and worldly way to flip him the finger. I laughed, understanding her actions. Drew poked her, and she ignored him.

"Anyway," she continued, pursing her lips to stop from smiling. "Chakra means wheels or discs or something. You have, like, at least seven wheels of energy in your body. Each one affects something different." She tapped the middle finger of her open right hand to her forehead. "Like the chakra that controls your third eye. It's your intuition."

"*I see dead people,*" Drew quoted from one of his favorite movies.

"Andrew C Shyamalan here kinda gets it." She otherwise didn't look at him to recognize his contribution. Drew laughed at the name mash-up. "It's your sixth sense."

I nodded, showing her that I was following along.

"Now, the energy that flows through your chakra is the prana. It's what keeps you healthy and stuff. When you don't take care of yourself, the energy in your chakra is depleted and it affects you physically."

"So I need more prana?" I asked, trying to keep track of the terms.

"You need the right amount of it," she corrected. "It's all about balance. Too little is bad. Too much is bad."

The philosophy of balance was something I could understand but the rest of this was an information dump.

"How do you balance it, then?"

She shrugged. "The right diet? Yoga? Meditation?" She straightened in her chair, closed her eyes, took a deliberate breath and let it out slowly. When she opened her eyes, they were brighter and stronger. "Breathe."

She picked up her spoon and started to eat again. She was smiling. If prana was real, she had more positive ones flowing through her chakras now.

"How do you know all this?" I finally asked, a bit overwhelmed and, honestly, partially impressed.

"I take yoga classes with my mom." She shrugged. "The teacher is cute."

First Day Back

Clear your mind.

Breathe.

I had been nightmare free for two nights. It may not necessarily have been Brieann's advice passed down from her cute yoga teacher that made the difference. But it probably didn't hurt to practice anyway.

But I wasn't going to sleep. I was going to school.

It was altogether a different kind of nightmare. One that I couldn't just wake up from. My anxiety was significantly higher.

A group of kids hanging out together outside of school is a party. The same group of kids confined together in a building is a reality TV show without the benefit of cameras or endorsements. High school.

I prepared for another round of unwanted attention and fake concern. And this time, I didn't have Ethan to hide behind.

"Maybe you can come to school with me," I proposed, desperately considering options. We were both sitting on the couch, not watching whatever it was that was playing on the screen.

Chase and Philip had stopped by a little before lunch to say goodbye. They took Liam with them when they left for the airport.

Locke's flight was later in the day; so he had stayed behind. That gave him a chance to have one more big meal on Dad's dime before he headed back to campus and resumed life as a broke college student.

I hated to see them all go. Not just because it was the official end to the extended holiday week but because it was also letting go of what I had always considered normal. Roles that made sense. Even with all the changes, just having everyone in the same place sharing a meal magically balanced life.

My family always grounded me. Always made me feel stable. I hadn't realized how much I missed that until experiencing it again reminded me.

Unintentionally, I might have transferred that anchoring responsibility to Ethan. Having him stay a little longer was good in so many ways. Delaying that departure gave me the chance to acclimate before yet another change to my foundation.

I knew that I should be facing this with the maturity of someone a year shy of being a legal adult. But I was feeling more like a kindergartener being told to leave my favorite stuffed bear behind for my first day of school.

I completed my whining request with big, pleading eyes.

It didn't sway him.

"Is it Take-Your-Kiwi-To-School Day?" he said with a laugh. I pouted.

He put his arm around my shoulder and pulled me to him. I allowed it and cuddled closer, my cheek on his chest.

"She'll be 'right," he assured me.

"What are you going to be doing all day while I'm in class anyway?" I asked, still with a whine. Still pouting. I felt his body shift in a casual shrug.

"Explore, I guess."

I was jealous. Jealous of the air around him that I wouldn't be able to share. It didn't help my mood.

He shifted again so that I had to sit up straight. He took his arm back from around me. I hated the feeling of being let go. But before I could wallow, he gently caressed my cheek. He waited until our eyes met.

"I'll be right here waiting for you," he promised. Then he kissed me.

I stopped pouting.

That was the night before. In the morning, I stood by Brieann's locker, waiting for her to dump her books in while I psyched myself.

"We're going to be late," I warned her.

"Chill," she said, taking the time to put on some lip gloss and retie her hair. She was right, of course. We had time. My anxiety was talking.

Clear your mind, I repeated to myself. *Breathe.*

She slammed her locker door and we walked down the hallway to Homeroom together.

That was when I was reminded that, despite my narrative, the whole world did not revolve around me.

Dance

The social politics of high school were as volatile as the raging hormones behind them. You could be a nobody one day and then the subject of unbelievable rumors the next. Suddenly everyone knew your name, what you had or didn't have for breakfast, and the last day of your period.

I was anticipating a nauseating rerun of being treated like the latest human oddity in the circus of freaks. It wouldn't be unfamiliar but unwelcome, nonetheless.

I forgot to consider the short attention span variable that can affect events exponentially. In this case, the apparent scandalous exploits over last Friday's party had them all forgetting about me.

Scrutiny of me evaporated completely.

But it dropped a combined ball of undeserved gossip all on Brieann's head.

Brieann was never a nobody but today, the only thing anybody cared about was who she was to Tristan. Or who she wasn't anymore.

Tristan's dramatic display had its desired effect. He made everything about him. Brieann was a strong, independent person so therefore, he must be the victim. It was immature and nasty. It was high school.

"I'm not sure being friends with me helps your case right now," I whispered to her as we took our usual seats next to each other. I tried to survey the room casually but everyone, literally everyone, was looking at her. Conversations even stopped and a couple of people weren't as subtle as they thought they were in pointing her out. As if there would be any mistake who the conversation was about.

"Don't you dare leave me," she responded more fiercely than I thought one could manage in a whisper.

"This seems like a good day to skip school," I suggested. Albeit, self-serving because that would mean we'd be hanging out with Ethan. I wasn't serious, but it was still nice to think about.

Mr. Jacobs walked in, staunch mechanical pencil behind one ear. He stopped next to us and put one hand on my desk. "Hey, hey, hey," he said. "Good to have you back with us Ms. Evans." Then louder, for the rest of the class, he said, "Show's over, minions. Thanksgiving weekend has officially ended, and we're back to the grind; so park it and let's Math."

Teachers always think they know what's going on. *The London Show* was so last season.

"So much for playing hooky, Ms. Evans," Brieann whispered. I put one finger up to my eye and traced an imaginary tear down my face.

It was Brieann's idea to spend our lunch period outside instead of wading through the cafeteria, thick with gossip. It wasn't like her to avoid confrontation, but I was all for it.

I have sat with Brieann's friends since the very first day of school. Not because I thought of them as my friends but just because that's where Brieann sat. I sat with her. She sat with them. They were friendly enough. Except Amanda. She had it in for me for whatever reason. It was baffling. It's not like we had any history together. She was just randomly foul. Maybe she didn't like my shoes. Maybe she didn't like my hair. Maybe she didn't like that a nobody from the Midwest would sit at the same table she did. We've never talked about it nor did I care enough about her to want to.

On a good day, I can stomach Amanda by pretending I was watching a bad reality show. On days like this one, her face was enough to make me puke.

We sat at one of the picnic tables under cherry blossom trees that were out of season. There were only a handful of other students in the quad with us. Likely, because temperatures had uncharacteristically dropped and it was starting to feel more like the Midwest than California. It didn't bother me so much, and it testified to Brieann's mood that it didn't seem to bother her either.

"What are you going to do?" I asked, hoping she had a plan of action. Because I didn't.

She stared up at the sky through the branches. She didn't look at me. "I don't actually really have to *do* anything. This is going to last, like, a week, if that." She shrugged. "At least until Tuesday."

"What's Tuesday?"

"Tuesday is when the Winter Formal Committee meets." She looked at me and smirked. "I'm the assigned Committee Chair; so if Amanda wants to be part of that, this will all just blow away."

She made fluttering motions with her fingers. There wasn't any celebration in that victory.

"Just like that?"

She sighed. "More or less." She looked up again. "There's a bigger dance that happens and it lasts all throughout high school. It starts in middle school. You dance with everyone, balancing schoolwork with fun. You learn who the good dancers are, and who really just wants to step on your feet. When you find someone you can dance with well, you stick together. The whole point is to make your way to the stage, where you get to be on top and see everything." She sighed. "It's a great view as long as you don't fall off."

"What if people want to push you off?" I asked. I could name names.

"Oh, so many people want to push you off," she laughed. "Most of the time, all you have to do is step to one side and let them topple themselves."

"This is like chess for high school relationships."

She flipped her hair over her shoulders. "I don't play chess." Then with a hint of mischief in her smile, she added, "But I know how to dance."

Drew had his Bologna Sandwich of Life Theory and Brieann had her Student Dance of High School Politics Algorithm.

She knew the dance well, and she was good at it.

"I'm just tired of it," she continued, her voice sounding just as fatigued. "It's a lot of effort for what? Like, what's even the point of it all? In a couple of years, we're all going to be doing our own things and actually starting life for real. We're probably not going to see most of these people until our 25th reunion or something." She twirled a strand of her hair around her finger. Her hair was straight today.

"I think this was really all more for survival, you know?" She looked at me for affirmation. "I just didn't want high school to suck."

"Tristan notwithstanding, I think you're rocking it. You know that." She had to know that. Brieann had to be the most popular girl in school, and we were't even seniors yet. That was the type of unmeasurable overachieving social attainment that attracted college scouts.

"Was it just too hot in the cafeteria?" Drew walked up to join us. He had his hands in his pockets and his shoulder's hunched. He had buttoned up his usually open green flannel.

"You could say that," I responded, watching him leap to sit on the table.

"I wasn't in the mood." Brieann was more direct.

Drew knew exactly why we were sitting outside. He had been inside and read the room. Like an undercover reporter, he was willing to share his intel. "The dirt is that you're a shallow tease and an ungrateful girlfriend. You think you're all that and then some. Poor, underappreciated Tristan just wasn't going to deal with that anymore." I grimaced at Drew's delivery. I'd have softened that blow before laying it down. I guess it wasn't his style. Brieann's lips tightened into a straight line. "I'm surprised that you aren't flushing the crap down before the flies circle," he added.

"I don't want to get my hands dirty. I think I'll just wait and let the flies get stuck in it or die on their own." There was more bitterness than fatigue in her words now.

"The shelf life for this is short," Drew agreed. "I think the Raven and Sam drama is going to cycle up to the top shortly."

"Honestly, I'd rather be called a prude than have people think that I was that into him," Brieann mumbled. It was consolation but it still hurt, either way.

"Here," Drew tossed a yogurt breakfast bar at her. She caught it in time and her face brightened. "They aren't worth missing a meal for."

She smiled at him and opened the fruity offering. "Sweet!" She broke off a piece to eat. Her mood visibly lightened.

I sat next to Drew on the table, bumping his shoulder with mine. He had the ability to make sucky situations better. "Well done," I said low enough so that Brieann didn't hear me. He grinned back at me.

"Just replenishing my cookie stash." According to Drew, the reward for all good deeds was not glory. He preferred cookies.

The hero yet again.

O, Christmas Tree

"How was the first day back to school?"

Deja vu.

Dad had reclaimed his office after my brothers left, sequestering Ethan back to the couch. That's where we were sitting when he came home. Ethan stood to greet him right away but I finished writing the answer to that last Trig problem before I got up to give Dad his customary greeting. He looked slightly annoyed that I had not dropped everything immediately to say hello. He was probably blaming Ethan for that in his head instead of my Math.

"Weird," I replied honestly.

Brieann did not act like herself all day. A conflict weighed on her that went beyond the superficial pageantry of high school. She had to decide on something but wouldn't divulge the question. Or maybe she didn't know what the question was. Either way, the motions of Monday were passed through a heavy filter.

Drew disappeared after lunch but showed up near Brieann's locker after the last period with a couple of his friends. He said they were there on behalf of the National Arts Honor Society to talk to her about the Winter Formal decorations or something to that effect.

I suspect he wanted to make sure that no one had an opportunity to bother her. It's always harder to prey on someone when they're part of a pack. He wanted to show everyone that Brieann was not alone.

Drew was well liked, but he didn't share Brieann's spotlight. They had overlapping friends but didn't run in the same circles. I thought it was because Drew didn't know how to play the game of social politics like Brieann. But today he proved that he was more familiar with the rules than I had thought. He just didn't care. It wasn't important enough to him.

It was important to Brieann, and that's why he played the game now.

I didn't know if Brieann realized what he was doing. Maybe she was just relieved that the opportunity presented itself.

I knew. I was already mentally baking cookies for Drew as his reward for being the hero she needed. He's racked up quite a batch.

"That's to be expected," Dad was saying, unperturbed by my response. "There's going to be an adjustment period but everything will fall into routine pretty quickly." Then with an air of innocence that was too thick to be genuine he added, "It's like riding a bike."

Considering that my attempt at getting back on a bike involved scratches on both myself and my bike, his analogy was both appropriate and strategically taunting. I stuck my tongue out at him. He smiled, content with the knowledge that his barb had hit its mark.

"What's for dinner?"

Dinner was significantly quieter with just the three of us at the table. There was nothing normal about the past week, but I fell into a comfortable pace with the hustle. It surprised me to realize that. I'm usually one to appreciate quiet over noise, but the cheer of genuine company was real.

"Have you heard from your brothers?" Dad asked between bites of the spaghetti I made for dinner. I had a bunch of homework to finish; so I opted for the quick and easy pasta with jarred sauce and sliced up hot dogs. That layer of cheese over everything had to work a little harder, but it did its job.

"They texted," I acknowledged. "Liam and Chase's flight was almost delayed but I guess it didn't snow when it was supposed to. They landed OK." I grabbed the bottle of hot sauce on the table and added a few drops to my meal. "Locke is hungry."

Dad snorted. They were all expected responses.

"Liam reminded me that tomorrow was the first of December," I said. Then after a pause, I asked, "Are we doing the whole decorations thing?"

Like Thanksgiving, this was going to be our first Christmas here. Most families I knew growing up set up their decorations over Thanksgiving weekend. Tree farms were big in the Midwest and hot apple cider was part of the tree picking ceremony. Our family didn't do real trees. We've had the same artificial tree since before I was born.

My parents bought that tree on their first Christmas together. It was top of the line at the time with built-in lights. That was almost three decades ago. There have been changes.

By the time I was born, the bulbs had burnt out and Dad had to remove them from the wire branches. We had a knitted tree skirt that covered up the duct tape on the legs. Liam added them when a crack in the plastic started to form. It was a preventive measure.

A little bit of the green fringe fell off every year. Dad and Liam had added new swag to it when I was 5. It gave it new life even if a little bit of green still fell off every year. It was a tree unlike any other.

This tree had gone from displaying glass-blown ornaments to child-made paper decorations held together with school glue to shatterproof balls that would bounce when they were shaken off. It had been crowned with angels, stars, and one Christmas, with a *Darth Vader* helmet. Sometimes it was lighted with white lights, sometimes colored. Every year was something different, and it endured.

The tree wouldn't be retired. That was a matter of pride.

Every December 1st, my brothers would assemble the tree and string up the lights. After so many years, it fell on me to trim the tree. Dad would sit on the couch and veto ideas. There was always hot chocolate. Usually from an instant powdered packet, but it was present. It became a family tradition.

This year, my brothers wouldn't be home. This year we might have the same old tree but we have a new house. It's another stage in the evolution process, but I couldn't envision how it would play out.

Dad didn't even hesitate. "Of course. Your brothers will be back for Christmas. We should have everything in place for that."

"Who is this 'we', *Kemosabe*?" Dad had grown comfortable with his position on the couch. There was no way he was going to give it up. I made a show of looking around. "You mean me and my one-handed friend here?"

Dad didn't miss a beat. "Invite more hands over then. Make an event out of it."

That wasn't a bad idea.

Past

"How did I get dragged into this again?" Drew was carrying another plastic bin into the living room. Two similar bins were already on the floor. Each one was labeled by color, indicating what kind of decorations were inside.

"I think hot chocolate was promised." Brieann opened up the nylon bag that held our Frankenstein tree. I had thrown an unused scented candle in with it last year, and the smell of pine was strong. "Honestly," she said to me. "I was expecting this to smell like moth balls. This is nice."

"I see no hot chocolate," Drew complained, still fixated on what was important to him. "I've been lied to."

"I figured you'd prefer a trip to *Caden's* after we're done here instead of the stale powdered mix in the back of our pantry." I helped Brieann gently extract the family artifact. Despite our efforts, some green fringe still fell to the floor.

Ethan was assembling the base. Not an easy task one-handed but he managed. He grinned at Drew. "Sucker," he said, just as I had before but with an accent.

Drew pointed a finger at him. "What the foreigner said. That's why I'm here. I'm a sucker." Despite his complaints, he went right back to the office for the rest of the bins. I was sure he preferred to do this over the History homework that he was *supposed* to be doing.

We had our lunch at the cafeteria today. Tristan and his point guards had already been sitting at the table with Amanda and Raven when we walked in. Brieann walked past them with the air of someone with great intention and sat at Drew's table with his friends.

The hype of what happened over Thanksgiving break had already worn itself out. With nothing new to add to the narrative, the whispering had stopped and attention was back to the Winter Formal coming up. The only people that seemed to have noticed Brieann's snub were Amanda and company.

I tried not to look overly enthusiastic. I much preferred Drew's crowd over Brieann's.

Then I asked them if they would help me after school. Eager to have an excuse, Brieann responded with enthusiasm. She was right. I may have mentioned hot chocolate without really committing to the promise.

Maybe I'll just bake Drew those cookies. He was certainly earning them.

It didn't take very long to get the tree itself set up. It was made up of only three pieces, if you didn't count the duct-taped legs. Our well-loved, battle-damaged tree still stood impressively straight after so many years. And it didn't look so sad after it was carefully fluffed. It fit well in the cluttered room. Ethan helped me wind the lights around it.

Drew was untangling outdoor lights. Another task that he got suckered into after Brieann started it and realized it wasn't as easy as she thought. She abandoned him to the chore and started to open other bins.

She made a half-squealing sound one would reserve for puppies and other helpless fuzzy animals when she held up a circular piece of cardboard adorned with my preschool picture. "Aren't you cute?" she exclaimed. "Look at your pigtails!"

Drew left his post to kneel next to her and join in the pillaging. This was artwork. Right up his alley. "Did you make this?" He picked up a grid of blue-painted Popsicle sticks in the shape of a snowflake … or what could pass off as a deadly weapon in any airline. Not the kind of thing that might impress a member of the NAHS.

"That was Locke's," I lied. I handed Ethan another strand of lights. "We don't use that bin anymore. It's filled with years of handmade holiday crafts that Dad is too sentimental to throw out."

Brieann was having too much fun to stop. She pulled out a wreath made with a dozen or so hand-shaped green construction paper cut outs. "Awwww, look at how small your hands were!" she exclaimed.

"A wreath of green children's hands. That's not creepy at all," Drew said behind her. She elbowed him.

"I think it's cute." She laid the paper wreath reverently on the floor beside her. "You should use these again. It would be a fun theme for your first Christmas here," she suggested.

Ethan joined them, interested to see pieces of my past. I found a second bin with the same color markings on them and opened it. It held paper chains stapled together. It was incredible that it had stayed fairly intact. I remembered the production line that my brothers had set up for this. Links were added at both ends at the same time while the other two would cut the construction paper to be used. We had completed it in record time; so that we could go sledding like Dad had promised. It was an achievement.

These flimsy physical objects cradle happy memories. Brieann was right. It was the perfect theme for this year's Christmas. Sometimes, she knew what she was talking about.

"That's a great idea, actually," I agreed. "Kinda like tying in the past with the present."

"It's a valid artist statement," Drew said, holding up a painted macaroni ornament.

"You have cards in here." Brieann picked up a handful of them, also showing them to Ethan. "And pictures too!"

Ethan took one of the photos. It was an old-fashioned Polaroid, yellowing with age. My brothers and I were sitting in front of the tree. We were dressed in matching pajamas. Liam was sitting cross-legged, smiling at the camera. He was holding the baby version of me on his lap. I can't have been a year old yet. I had my fingers in my mouth and drool dripping down one chubby arm. Next to us, Chase was hugging Locke, probably to keep him from running away. On the back of the picture, someone had scrawled "Liam, Lincoln, Locke, and London ~ Christmas eve". It was in cursive with a blue pen. It was not Dad's penmanship.

"You were a chubby ankle biter, weren't you?" Ethan teased.

"I was a cute baby!" I laughed, taking the photo from him.

Brieann was holding another photo. "Oh, hey, London. Is this your Mom?" She flipped it around to show me.

The smiling woman in the photo wasn't looking at the camera. She was distracted. Her long, brown hair came straight down past her shoulders. It partially covered the chubby ankle biter that she was looking down on.

"Well, I think that's me; so that's probably her." I held out my hand so I could take the picture from her. Brieann looked at it one more time before handing it over.

"She's pretty," she said. "I think she looks like you."

I held the Polaroid in my hand and studied the faded picture closer. The baby, wearing a warm holiday onesie that was a size too big, was definitely me. Fingers of one hand still in the mouth and the other reaching for the woman.

The woman, eyes on the baby, wore what looked like a light long-sleeved sweater. And around her shoulders was a knitted shawl in mostly shades of violet.

I was hit with an unexpected realization. The force of it was an iced snowball to my face. I scrambled to my feet, unable to put into words what I was thinking. The head rush that followed my sudden movement added to shakiness. I was light-headed and unstable. The last thing I remember seeing was the alarmed faces of my friends before everything turned white.

Trance

The sun was up higher than it should have been, but it was just as cold. I tasted bile in my throat and thought that I'd have to experience the spicy nachos from lunch all over again. I took necessary big gulps of air and was able to defer the disaster.

The alley didn't look as forbidding in the daylight but still just as desolate. The ground seemed damp despite the concrete's lighter color. To be fair, there was nothing especially objectionable about the space. It was very much like a homogeneous back alley that was standard in every big city.

But I knew what waited for me, making this otherwise meaningless area particularly unwelcome.

I didn't bother to zip up my hoodie. The ends lashed around my waist almost in slow motion. Everything suddenly felt very, very slow.

I saw the knitted shawl first. The colors were brighter in the light but otherwise still worn, almost as if the yarn itself was faded. The shelter protected it from the wind but it still danced a little, pulling away from the figure it was wrapped around.

I walked toward the shelter with more purpose than I had before.

The shawl shifted and revealed her face.

Her eyes were closed and she was not smiling. She was a ghost of what she used to be. I could see her now in the sunlight with eyes fresh from visiting the past.

She opened her eyes, and it was the first time I was certain of myself.

She might have moved. She might have said something. I wouldn't know because, just as suddenly, I was already gone.

Unmasked

I felt a cold, damp paper towel on my forehead. My eyes opened. I saw the deep concern on Ethan's face as he cradled me on his lap. We were on the couch, my feet propped up with pillows.

"She's waking up," Brieann announced. I looked to the direction of her voice and was greeted with a glass of water. I didn't take it right away. Ethan took the paper towel off me. I sat up. Strands of wet hair stuck to my forehead. It felt gross. I swung my feet off the couch.

"What happened?" I asked, finally taking the glass that Drew offered.

"I think you fainted," Drew said. "I've seen this before but at least this time, it looks like you aren't bleeding." He gestured to the scar on my arm.

Ethan's face deepened into a troubled frown. I leaned against him more to assure him than for support. I compared the experiences in my head and answered carefully.

"Something was the same, yeah. But it was also different." I paused to consider the variables. "I don't have a migraine or anything this time. I was feeling totally fine. It was just a head rush." I looked at Ethan for emphasis. "I feel totally fine now."

He didn't look convinced.

"Really, I do." My voice was stronger, and I was confident. "For just that few minutes, I just got really lightheaded." I grasped at the air trying to find the words to describe it accurately. "Like falling down a rollercoaster and your stomach isn't where it's supposed to be."

"Did you *skip*?" Ethan's voice was cautious. A reminder of what it had been in the middle of a desperate situation. The little hairs on my arms ran up all the way to the back of my neck like a scared rabbit, making me shiver once.

"Yes."

When I didn't offer anything else, Brieann prodded. "What did you see?"

My eyes flickered instinctively to the Polaroid abandoned on the floor. It was face-up where I dropped it. A captured moment between a woman and her daughter. A woman, who didn't keep her hair but kept the shawl.

"I saw her."

The same shawl. The same woman.

Brieann looked first at Drew. He shook his head. She looked back at me. "What does that mean?"

It meant the thing in my nightmares was my mother.

History

Even though Drew and Brieann waited to leave until right when Dad got home, we didn't really make a lot of progress getting the decorations up. Other than a string of lights, the tree was still bare. Open and unopened bins covered most of the floor. The best we could do was clear a path from the front door through to the kitchen.

I was shaken by the experience of the last dream. Any holiday spirit I might have had going through old memories was replaced with troubled anxiety. There were other things on my mind.

"We need to talk."

That was how I greeted Dad when he walked through the door, his coat over his arm and holding a half-empty box of faculty donuts.

I took the box from him and set it dismissively on top of an unopened bin while he hung up his coat. He had a very uncertain smile on his face, probably to counteract what he knew was something unpleasant coming his way, even if he didn't know the cause.

"Uh oh," he said with forced humor. "That's never a good thing."

Ethan was strategically absent. He sat in the cluttered living room with the TV on, feigning disinterest. It didn't matter if he was unconvincing. It was enough that he pretended. Otherwise, Dad would never talk.

I gestured to the office, hoping that he'd feel more comfortable in his own space. He went ahead and I followed.

"What's going on?" he asked directly when I had closed the door.

"Tell me about Mom," I said, still facing the door. I heard him sigh and shift around the room. I didn't turn around until he spoke again.

"Is there something specific about her that you want to know?" Dad didn't play games about things that mattered to me. It was one of the reasons talking to him was so easy. He knew something important was happening here.

He sat in his office chair, an arm's length away from the table. I cleared the mug of coffee that should have probably been in the dishwasher two days ago and sat on the table so we were close to each other. This was an intimate subject. I didn't want a whole lot of space between us.

"How did she die?"

There was a sharp intake of breath, and he blinked rapidly for a few seconds. It was a sign of concealed panic. Then his eyebrows came down and his voice took the stern tone he reserved for drawing lines I shouldn't dare cross.

"I don't want to talk about this." There was a warning in his words. It was at that moment that I realized all that I thought I knew about my mother had been sugar coated and possibly straight up lies. He was hiding something.

I needed to know what that was.

"I do," I insisted, just as strongly, meeting his gaze unflinchingly. He did not respond immediately.

"What brought this on?" he asked, heavy with suspicion. "Was it something your boyfriend said?"

He said the word *boyfriend* with contempt. It was my turn to bristle. I had to bite back a response when I recognized it for what it was. Deflection. It was a tactic that might have worked had I not been so stubborn. I could see it clearly. He was trying to find an escape.

I had never seen him like this. He was acting like a 3-year-old caught with a permanent marker and a jacked-up wall. It would have been comical if not for the severity of this conversation. He was hiding something. And if he was this uncomfortable, it must be something truly distasteful. Or painful. I felt bad for him.

I would have let him off the hook but if a trade was necessary, then so be it. I couldn't stay ignorant any longer. I softened my tone.

"Something happened today and I need to know that I'm not crazy," I said softly, appealing to his protective nature. We were just starting to recover from our own kind of hell recently. Me, thinking that Ethan had died and him, not understanding what was driving me mad.

"What happened?" he asked, no longer defensive.

"You first," I insisted. I could not back down.

I had won every argument we've ever had since I was young. My brothers complained that it was because I reminded him so much of my mother. Add being the youngest and the only girl into the equation had everything stacked in my favor. I was banking on all that now. And I threw in my recent anguish into the fray for extra measure.

He took his time, assessing my resolve. Ultimately, it worked. He leaned back on his chair, shoulders slumped like he was too tired to sit up straight.

"What do you know about what happened to your mother?" he asked. He wasn't trying to distract me this time. He wanted to know how much I *didn't* know.

I knew very little. It hadn't occurred to my ignorant little self that I needed to know more.

"She had pneumonia? She died when I was, like, 9 months old or something?"

The guilty sadness in his eyes told me that I was wrong even before he spoke.

"You were about to be 9 months old," he corrected. Now that the truth was coming out, it might as well be as accurate as possible. "And it wasn't pneumonia."

He paused and searched my eyes. I didn't know what he was seeking exactly. I didn't know if he found it. He reached for my hands and held both of mine between his. The delicate chain of Ethan's bracelet rested on my wrist. He rubbed his thumb over it once, deep in thought. He stumbled over his words.

"I wasn't prepared to raise all of you by myself," he said. "I wasn't prepared to lose your mother so early." It wasn't what I was asking but he knew that. I didn't say anything.

"I suppose no one really ever is. When you plan the rest of your life together with someone, you don't expect to continue on your own." His words exposed a vulnerability that he would rarely admit, if he would admit it at all. A father provides an impenetrable sense of safety. That was a father's job. And this was a very weak spot in his armor.

"I didn't do a very good job adjusting after," he admitted with woeful regret. "It took me so long. I just … I missed her so much. It was a very difficult time in my life. In all our lives, really, but I hoped that it didn't seem that way."

I couldn't speak for my brothers. Apart from Locke, who was also just a toddler when it happened, they knew of a life with her and then without her. I've only known a world that told stories *about* her.

It never bothered me. Not in the way that people always seemed to expect that it would. I suppose imagining the what-ifs was normal. But it was also in the same category as most kids would dream of being royalty or a superhero. My childhood was great. I never felt like I was missing out.

"I hope that it was enough. I hope *I* was enough. That I was a good enough father *and* mother to you."

"Oh, Dad," I finally said because he needed the assurance before he could continue. "That's not what this is about."

He nodded right away, knowing it wasn't. It was more like a disclaimer before he could say what he had to say.

"Sweetheart," he said gently. "You need to understand that there were a lot of factors involved. There are a lot of questions that we never found the answers to. I can tell you everything I know but it might not be what you're looking for. "

I was very confused and also slightly afraid, but I didn't interrupt.

"Sometimes, in this world, that happens. You don't always get the explanations you deserve."

"I still want to know," I insisted, but my voice had lost its edge.

"I know you do, Sweetheart. You're old enough. You're mature enough. It's time. It's just … I don't know if I want this for you yet."

We sat there for a very long minute, just father and daughter holding hands while the whole world paused. The minute stretched so long that I felt I could see the thin lines in the space between the conflict in Dad's head. He was already arguing with himself and he didn't need me to kick up the dirt. I wanted to join the debate. I wanted to push. Something held me back. He had to get there on his own. He needed me to let him. So I waited.

It was the right thing to do.

A new resolve steadied his voice, though it remained soft. "There are a few things that I'm sure of. One, is that your mother *loved* you. She loved your brothers, of course. No one could love them more. But *you*," he patted my hands. "You, she was waiting for."

It was a sweet sentiment. Almost expected. I nodded to let him know that even though I was impatient, I was also listening.

"Two, is that none of this was your fault."

That I was not expecting. I almost pulled my hands away.

Not my fault?

Not *my* fault?

Not my fault?

It never occurred to me that anything that had happened to my mother was my fault. But when it was phrased like that, it certainly sounded like *something* was. Maybe not everything, but something. Where did the emphasis lie?

What could have possibly happened? Did she have to run into a burning building to save me? Was I playing in the middle of traffic that she had to step in front of a speeding car so that I wouldn't be turned into roadkill? Did I toss a toaster in her bathwater? Did I *kill* her?

Theory after theory was increasingly ridiculous. I was spiraling away from possibilities and into straight-up fantasy fiction.

"Do you understand?"

No. No, I didn't.

But I nodded my head anyway because I wanted him to continue. Somehow, it satisfied him and he did.

"It was the first winter after you were born. Bitter. Especially that day. *That* day was cold as hell." His eyes shifted focus. It was not affected by distance but by time. He was remembering and it was that exact moment he was really seeing.

"It was awful outside. We had just been hit by one of the worst blizzards in recorded history. Some people lost power. School was out. The roads were nasty. I left work early and it still took me over twice as long to get home. When I finally *did* get home, I found out that your Mom had asked Lorna to watch your brothers. Mrs. Bautista? Remember her?" I nodded, still silent.

She was our next door neighbor. I used to stop by her house everyday after school until they moved away when I was 8. She used to sneak me M&Ms when Dad wasn't looking.

"You were still a baby; so I guess maybe your Mom thought it made sense that she took you wherever she was going." He shook his head, like he didn't believe what he was saying. "But she didn't say where she was going. I thought that maybe there was some errand she forgot to do. Something important that made sense to go out when conditions were so bad. Maybe the doctor? Pick up a prescription? The bank? I don't know."

My hands should've been warm with my dad having held them so long, but they had turned clammy. There was an uncomfortable tightening in my stomach. I held my breath to keep myself from wanting to throw up. I didn't like this conversation any more than he did.

"I tried to call her but it just kept going to voicemail. I couldn't find her. I called people she worked with … her friends … no one knew where she had gone." His voice cracked. He looked so helpless and my heart ached for him. "She was gone all night. I couldn't sleep. Worst night of my life."

This was so difficult for him and I felt guilty. I squeezed his hands, reminding him that we were talking about the past and it wasn't what was happening now. He didn't continue right away. And when he started again, his voice was just over a whisper.

"We didn't hear anything until the next afternoon." He looked right at me, his eyes sadder than I've ever seen them before. I swallowed painfully and realized that I already had tears in my own eyes.

"I got a call from the Department of Family Services." He looked down at our hands, and I was glad for it because I wasn't sure if I could stop myself from crying. Not because he was telling me about how I lost my mother but because he was telling me about the most painful moments of his life. When he lost the woman he loved.

He loved my mother so deeply that even though I never knew her, their relationship was the standard I held every relationship to. He loved her in a way that taught me what love is. In a way that most people don't know is even possible. And now, he was reliving losing her again. He was feeling every raw emotion he had felt then. It was destructive.

"Your Mom's car got stuck in the snow. Battery was completely dead. Firefighters had rescued you. They found you in her arms. Perfectly safe."

When he looked up again, he was crying but he had a smile on his face. Almost one of pride. His voice shook but there was resolution in them. A truth that can never be shaken by grief or pain. "Your mother did everything in her power to keep you warm. Whatever it took. That's how much she loved you."

That's when I realized what he was saying. That's when I realized what he meant when he said that it wasn't my fault.

Faced with the worst of conditions she couldn't control, my mother did what she *could* do. She made sure that I was warm. She made sure that I was safe.

My mother died because she wanted to make sure that I lived.

From the Ashes

"I never knew."

I was crying again. Ethan put his arm around me, and I leaned against him, not caring that I was ruining his shirt. Brieann had both hands up to her mouth and her eyes were shining with tears. Drew was standing in front of me, his hands in his pockets, his face solemn.

We had taken over one of the big tables meant for families. Most of the park was empty even though the weather was warmer than it had been for days. Californians had a low tolerance for cold.

I refused to think about this in school. If I started, I might not have been able to stop. The result would be tears. That wasn't a very agreeable state while trying to balance Chemical equations or Trigonometry functions.

Instead, Ethan and I met Drew and Brieann at the park after school. It was close enough and, more importantly, empty. It was a neutral location where we could talk more freely about the night before.

After Dad and I had talked, I sat unmoving, slowly processing the ramifications of his revelation. He had kissed me on the forehead and excused himself, mumbling something about having forgotten something in his car.

Ethan had walked in shortly after, knocking softly on the open door. He put a hand on me gently, almost questioningly. It was what I needed to be able to move again.

I fell into his embrace, sobbing. I wasn't sure exactly why I was crying. Just a little of the burden my father had been carrying for my entire life was enough to dismantle me. He was right. There was so much we didn't know even when the weight of what we did know was already staggering.

Dinner was late. Both Dad and I were still a little sore around the eyes. It was the only indication of our encounter. We spent the rest of the evening acting like it was any other school night. Ethan was our buffer. He fielded our polite questions on puzzling New Zealand slang words and pop culture references. He didn't talk about his life in the barracks. We didn't ask. We kept the conversation light.

It was a strain, nonetheless. Dad retired to his room earlier than usual, leaving me alone with Ethan. It would have been a good time to take advantage of the privacy. But we just sat on the couch together, ignoring whatever was on the screen in front of us. I would play with his hand absentmindedly and he would kiss my hair.

Having him there, even without saying anything, built me back up.

I thought about how Dad was alone.

"Did your brothers know?" Drew was asking.

I untangled myself slowly from Ethan, wiping my eyes with the back of my sleeve, trying to be dignified and failing. "I don't know. If anyone knew, it would probably just be Liam. Locke was too young and I don't see my Dad telling Chase."

"I can see why they didn't tell you though. That's ... that's a lot."

"I don't understand," Brieann said.

"That's not something you really tell a kid, Bree," Drew admonished. "Not if you don't want to have to pay for some serious therapy."

"I go to therapy," Brieann dismissed him. "Everyone should. It's like having regular dentist visits. It's healthy regardless of any cavities."

I smiled at her. She was never the type to judge so easily and I loved how nonchalantly she made Drew see that he was being presumptuous. Drew held up both his hands in surrender.

"But that's not what I mean," she clarified. "I mean, I don't understand your *skipping*. You dream of Ethan and it turns out everything you were dreaming was real. That alone is straight up science fiction or something, but OK, I accept that. I get it. Sort of."

She leaned forward on the bench, rocking it a little. "How could you be dreaming of your Mom if she died 16 years ago?"

"You sure it is your Mom, right?" Drew asked me the same question yesterday when I told them what I saw during my fainting spell. I answered him more than once already; so this time, I just gave him a side eye.

"Maybe it's not just distance. Maybe you *skip* through time too," Ethan suggested.

"That makes the most sense, actually," Brieann agreed thoughtfully. "We don't know how any of this works."

"She looked different though," I countered. "Not like in the picture. I mean, I'm sure it's her. She even had the same exact shawl." I didn't doubt that. "But she had absolutely no hair. And she looked … gaunt?" I was struggling to find the right adjectives.

"What if you *skip* through dimensions?" I checked to see if Drew was teasing me but his suggestion was just as genuine as the others. He sat next to Brieann on the table. "Like, what if you *skip* to different levels of hell, or something."

I was offended. "You think my Mom is in hell?" After having made the ultimate sacrifice, that didn't make any sense at all.

He held his hands up again. "You're the one having nightmares. I don't think nightmares are one of heaven's selling points."

He had a point but I was still annoyed.

"Maybe it's a type of purgatory?" Brieann moderated. "Or, like, an alternate world?"

Drew clung to that idea, possibly to get him out of the sensitive hole he unwittingly fell into. "Do you think you're seeing her spirit?"

I didn't know what ghosts were supposed to look like. Ashen? Wispy? Transparent? While she did look weak and pale, when she had grabbed me, her hold was solid. I would have been convinced that she was a completely corporeal being but there was something mercurial about her presence in my dreams. Like a bad connection. I didn't know if that was my fault or hers.

"Do you think she's trying to tell me something?" I asked in a very small voice. "What?"

"She's already told you plenty," Ethan observed. He held my hand. "Because of these *skips*, you've learned more about her than you have known all your life. It's a gift."

"A gift that hurts like hell," I complained.

There was truth in the adage that ignorance is bliss. Seventeen years I've lived without knowing the cost for my existence. I didn't feel the guilt or responsibility. That was a comfort that I didn't know I had.

But there is power in knowledge. I didn't want to admit it too easily, but he was right. I feel like there was an actual connection between this woman I've never known and me. I wasn't looking for one but found this anyway. It was painful but it was also uniquely empowering. My mother was a strong woman capable of selflessness and sacrifice. Part of her lived in me. I had that power too.

"Do you think you'll dream of her again?"

I shrugged. I wasn't ready to be done with my self-imposed pity party. "It's not like I've ever really been able to control all this."

"Oh? You mean haven't reigned in your swirling wheels of energy?" Drew asked, making circular motions with his hands.

"You're making fun of me!" Brieann accused. His grin was confirmation. She swatted him playfully. He pretended to cower.

"Zen!" he yelled at her. "Zen yourself!"

"I'll show you Zen …" she threatened, standing up so that she would have more leverage when she tried to poke and pinch him. He ran away. She chased him.

The pity party was over. I smiled at their banter. Ethan looked down at me, relieved to see that I stopped crying.

"I should try it," I told him. "The whole meditation thing. Maybe then it'll be easier to keep in touch with you when you leave."

He shook his head, amused. "The Internet does exist in New Zealand, yeah?" I wasn't appeased. "Let's review," he said. "In addition to the traditional ways of communicating like snail mail that generations before us have successfully made use of …

sometimes even in the middle of war … there is also email, text messaging, social media …" he counted the different ways on his fingers.

I interrupted his tirade with a kiss. "But if I could skip to you, we could actually do this," I pointed out. He sighed.

"I just don't like that there are too many things we don't understand about it," he said. "It's bad enough that there's a danger that you could be hurt while you're *skipping*. What if this is killing you and you don't even know it?"

"Killing me?"

"Little by little," he clarified. "Like smoking would."

I hadn't thought about that. What if he was right? What if that's what happened to Mom? What if she just … ran out of juice? I frowned.

He pulled me close to him and kissed my hair. "I'm not worried about us staying connected. Have you not realized this yet, London? The universe would have to implode to keep us apart."

Powder

The cement might have been dark gray with grime. It might have even been sticky with layers of colorful bodily fluid. I wouldn't know because it was covered with layers of heavy snow. And there was more of it steadily falling.

I could feel the ice melting inside my shoes. I alternated pulling one foot up and then the other as if it would make any difference. It didn't, of course. The snow covered everything. Including me.

I pulled the hood of my thin hoodie over my head. Any kind of barrier was better than nothing. It helped. It was already warming the back of my neck. I brushed the melting flakes off my face and blinked repeatedly to clear them from my lashes.

It wasn't even that cold, really. Maybe just a little colder than it had been in the park. It was just so much *whiter*.

I was not in the park, clearly. The alley that I've come to expect was transformed under this frost blanket. It brightened the unwelcoming darkness and softened harsh lines. The snow made promises of hot chocolate with marshmallows and colorful sprinkles. It was the kind of snow that manufacturers hoped to capture in festive globes to take to places that have never experienced snow. You could almost imagine the individual crystals that made up the fat flakes.

It was the snow of my childhood.

I felt a pit in my stomach where nostalgia and recent revelations clashed. This used to be enchanting. Snow used to mean promises of winter magic. It meant something different now. Something darker. Something cursed.

I pulled my hands into my sleeves like I have done innumerable times when I had forgotten to bring gloves. Or if I were just too lazy to. Then I scooped up a small amount to pack into a tiny snowball.

Perfect packing snow. That was what was falling from the sky. Heavy and deadly.

I left impressions in the snow when I walked. There was none entering the alley. They began where I had started walking.

No longer afraid, I approached the shelter where I knew she waited.

Her head was bare. The snow was not falling in the shelter; so there was no trace of it on her. But she was curled on the ground, her shawl tangled in a ball beneath her arms.

I reached out to touch her, hesitating only for a moment in anticipation of what I might actually feel. She felt real.

She opened her eyes and turned her head to me. It was a reaction to my touch but instead of looking at me, she was looking through me. There was an eerie gravity in her expression. One of urgent importance but timeless.

"This is not the end." Her voice echoed in my chest.

The cold got to me. I shuddered. I didn't know how to respond. "Mom?" I asked instead. The word was foreign in my mouth. I had never used it in my life. It felt forced.

She didn't hear me. Her voice was the most composed it had ever been. Almost reasonable. But the voice still wasn't speaking to me.

"I can't. I tried but it's gone. It doesn't matter." She leaned her head on her shawl. "They won't find her."

"Mom?" I tried again. It was still out-of-place but also necessary. "What are you trying to tell me, Mom?" I knelt down next to her, trying to hear her better. She didn't respond. I felt helpless. Helpless and useless.

When I had skipped to see Ethan, I hadn't paid much attention to my surroundings. The result of my inattentiveness was that I thought he lived in another universe instead of a different country.

My nightmares had paralyzed me with fear, but I wasn't afraid anymore.

I looked up to get an idea of where we were. The sky was dropping so much snow that I couldn't see past it. The immediate surroundings weren't particularly defining other than being a uniform big city back alley. We could have been in *Gotham City* or behind the apartment buildings of *Sesame Street*.

The absence of a grouchy, green monster in a trashcan did suggest that we probably weren't on the set of *Sesame Street*.

I stood up, not bothering to brush the snow off my jeans. I took another look at Mom. I hesitated leaving her but doing so would probably help us both.

"I'll be right back," I promised, not even considering that it may very well be a lie.

My Chucks slipped on the wet snow. They weren't meant for this weather. It forced me to slow down. Even so, I made it quickly to the end of the backstreet.

It opened up to another tight alley. Yellow street lights illuminated the falling snow more than it did the street. Low metal fences surrounded empty flower beds meant to be blooming on other days when it wasn't snowing.

The streets were empty. A couple of cars were parked along the sidewalk but were already draped in snow. Construction scaffolding hung abandoned on the side of a building. Underneath it was a temporary walkway to protect the sidewalk from debris. Another building had a big sign advertising parking. There were no other footprints but mine.

Further along, I heard traffic. I pivoted and half-ran as fast as I dared toward the noise. As I got closer to the intersection, it seemed that snow eased, or perhaps the light was brighter. I could see cars speeding down what was at least a four lane boulevard. Not just signs of civilization but signs of a well-populated city.

Just as I got to the corner, I stumbled. Not because of my sneakers. I was doing a good job balancing between sliding on the ice and running. I fell because I had missed the edge of the sidewalk. The snow had covered both the street and the sidewalk in an even layer. When I put my full weight on what I thought was still the sidewalk, the snow gave way. My ankle landed in a bad angle, and my knee buckled. I caught myself with my hands outstretched in front of me, and slid forward until my chin was in dirty snow and slush.

I scrambled backward, afraid that I had slid into the middle of the road. The boulevard was wide, with plenty of runoff. I wasn't in any danger of getting run over, but my dignity was probably roadkill.

I sat on the snow, my back to the cement of the building. I tested my ankle in slow circles while trying to catch my breath. Adrenaline was pounding my heartbeat in my ears. I got to my feet before the snow could melt through the seat of my jeans.

The lights were definitely brighter here. There were tall ones in the middle of the boulevard, arching over the road. The ones on the wide sidewalk had six globes in each one, scattering yellow light around them. The large windows of the buildings had their lights on, even when their doors were shuttered.

Where I stood, the buildings were built shoulder to shoulder. So close together that they shared a wall. The only way you could tell one ended and the other began was the obvious change in architecture. To one side, bright red awnings provided shade to possible patrons of the restaurant. Red and green twinkling lights ran around the windows. Potted evergreens looked like little towers of snow. Christmastime in the city.

In contrast, across the busy boulevard, a wide stone bridge arched forward into what seemed like an empty space. The towers of the bridge were massive, monolithic blocks of stone. The snow highlighted the heavy carvings that adorned it. On either side, reaching like a lazy stretch, were perfectly manicured parks. Stone flower pots were trimmed with festive decorations and string lights.

The intersection light turned red and a bright green symbol of a walking man indicated the right of way to cross. I looked both ways, not fully trusting of my environment. There were only three cars on the street, and they were stopped. I crossed tentatively at first and then hurried when the green walking man turned into a red countdown.

After I safely crossed, I looked up at a bronze statue of a rider on a rearing horse. I hadn't quite made it to the foot of the bridge, but the parks had leveled the ground and made it easier to see past the sides of homogeneous buildings.

Taller buildings in the distance cut the horizon and lost their height in the clouds. The cityscape was breathtaking. Traditional stone towers stood next to more modern high-rises. One looked like it was a massive pillar. Another seemed to be made entirely of glass, reflecting the sky and city lights. But the one that caught my attention had a sloped diamond shaped top, outlined in lights. It was iconic and I knew what it was. I knew it well.

I knew *where* I was.

Chicago.

Bad Idea

"Chicago?" Brieann repeated in disbelief.

"Maybe you dreamt Chicago because of what your Dad said," Drew suggested. "Dreams are like that, right? They're influenced by stuff that you experience when you're awake. Or, like, stuff you ate."

"That's true for regular dreams but this wasn't a regular dream," I argued.

"You sure you were *skipping*?" He was still doubtful.

I put my foot on the bench and pulled up the hem of my jeans just so that he could see the faint bruise on my ankle. "I landed badly in my dream. Woke up to major swelling."

"This is why *skipping* isn't a good idea," Ethan warned again. His butterfly knife was spiraling in his hand. I hadn't seen him holding it since the night he arrived. But after our conversation this morning, he hadn't let go of it.

It had made both Brieann and Drew nervous when he had first started flipping it in front of them. Ethan forgets that most people see it for the weapon it is and not his personal fidget spinner. The beautifully maintained blade was sharp and unforgiving, clearly not a novelty. The handles were artistically carved but obviously well used. By itself, the knife already looked intimidating in its elegance. In Ethan's hands, it was threateningly deadly.

He had to tone it down and explain himself. It took several assurances from us both and a short demonstration of his abilities before they were convinced that it was safe enough for them to be within six feet of him. Even so, every time the blade flashed, Drew would shift uncomfortably.

Sometimes Ethan flipped it; other times he just let it spin in a lazy circle. It was almost directly proportional to his emotions.

"Ouch," Drew flinched in reaction to my swelling ankle.

"It got me out of gym today, at least." I dropped my pant leg and foot to the ground.

"Good for you. Stupid burpees," Brieann complained. "I wonder why they call them burpees," she wondered, distracted.

"Because it sounds better than *pukees*?" I suggested.

"Pukees *are* more accurate."

"Reasons-to-hate-gym-ees? My-heart-feels-like-its-about-to-explode-ees? Why-does-the-world-hate-me-ees?"

"Yeah, they don't roll off the tongue quite as easily."

"Were you back in time?" Drew asked, unaffected by our tangent.

"I don't know," I admitted. "It's not like there was a date stamp or anything. But there was snow and it was Christmastime so it felt like now?" I couldn't be sure.

Drew nodded in understanding. "Too bad you didn't see a newspaper or something. That's how kidnappers do proof of life. They take a picture with the day's paper. Makes it all current."

"It bothers me that's your takeaway from all this," Brieann told him. He grinned.

"I won't know unless I actually *go* there. Like, go there from *here*. Not go there by *skipping*." I had talked this over with Ethan, and he wasn't very enthusiastic about my conclusion any more than he approved of my *skipping*. Hence the spinning knife. "I know exactly what alley she's in from my dream. I know I can find it."

I may have grown up in the suburbs, but I had spent enough weekends in the city. The bridge I had seen the cityscape from was a significant landmark. It would be so easy to work backward from there. Even in the snow.

"What? You're just going to fly there over the weekend?" Drew said incredulously.

"Yes," I said with equal confidence. "Exactly that."

"Do you have any idea how much that's going to cost?"

That was what Dad said when I told him. I scowled. "You sound like my Dad," I complained.

"He's not wrong. Smart man, your Dad."

"I have to go," I insisted.

"Reality check, London."

"You don't understand."

"No, I don't. And neither do you! Nothing about this makes any sense and you know it."

Our voices were getting increasingly louder, trying to beat each other's argument by volume instead of making any point. Drew was dismissing anything I said, and that was aggravating me more. We went at it for a few more rounds while Brieann silently watched our exchange. Her forehead wrinkled up and her face was serious.

"What are you going to do?" she finally interrupted in a quiet, level voice.

I turned my back on Drew to face her. I knew it was unnecessary but it made Drew mad. That was why I did it. He made a noise behind me, understanding that I was being just as dismissive with my actions as he was with his words. It was fair play as far as I was concerned.

"I'm going." I had already made up my mind. The argument I was having with Drew wasn't changing anything. "I mean, *we're* going," I amended. Ethan had momentarily paused flipping his knife so I put my hand over his, preventing him from opening it again. He didn't meet my eyes. "Tomorrow. I already bought tickets online."

"WHAT?" Drew was just as happy as Ethan was. "I can't believe your Dad thought it was a good idea."

Ethan made a noise and I glared at him, tightening my grip on his hand. Drew looked from him to me and interpreted things correctly. He pointed at me knowingly. "You didn't tell your Dad," he accused.

"Oh, that's not a good idea," Brieann said right away. She stood up to emphasize her point. "No, not a good idea. Your Dad is *not* going to like that."

My friends were good people. They were responsible, straight-laced students that knew the rules and followed them without complaint. Arguably, they were being much better children to their parents than I was being to my Dad. Heck, they were being better children to *my* Dad at this point.

"You can't possibly think this is a good idea," Drew said to Ethan, pulling him into the argument. It wasn't that they were ganging up on me, I knew that. They meant well. It was more of an intervention. I appreciated their concern. I really did. It was a testament to what good friends they were. But I felt like they also couldn't understand where I was coming from.

They both had their parents. They both had normal, stable families. They had all their questions answered on a fundamental level.

All I had were more questions. It wasn't that I was being a rebellious teenager. I wasn't acting out because the world was unfair. I just wanted to understand the truth and this was the next step to take.

"Look," I said, before Ethan could respond. "I know this is all crazy. I know It doesn't make much sense to you." Drew opened his mouth and I pointed at him sharply to indicate that I wasn't done talking. He crossed his arms in front of him, but stayed silent. "I don't know what these dreams mean. I don't know if I'm *skipping* to the past or to some alternate dimension. I don't know why, and I don't know why *now*."

I had lowered my voice to a reasonable level and tried to speak without letting my frustration influence my tone. "This is how I think of it. Best case scenario, I find her, right? Best case scenario, she's reaching out to me right here. Right now. Not some parallel universe like I thought Ethan was a part of, but, like, *this* world. Just like Ethan. I don't know how it's possible, but I can't really argue about what isn't possible anymore, now can I?" I gestured at Ethan to make my point. His existence alone was against reason.

"I may not have known her she *is* my mother. My brothers and I have lived most of our lives without one. I don't even know what it's like otherwise." Both Drew and Brieann lowered their eyes. They were guilty of being more fortunate. I didn't set out to make them feel bad but this was helping my cause so I kept going.

"What if she's alive? What if she needs my help? I'm supposed to just ignore that because it's "impossible"?" I put air quotes around the word just to be more sarcastic. "I'm talking about getting *on* a plane, not jumping *off* one. Yes, it's a lot of money but don't you think I owe it to myself? Don't you think I owe it to my Dad to do my best to find out?"

No one was smiling at me, but no one was arguing either. "Worst case scenario," I said just so they knew that I considered it too. "I blow a few hundred dollars, and Dad grounds me for the rest of my life." I paused to let it sink in.

"I still think that it's worth the chance."

It was quiet. At least the arguing had stopped. It was replaced with a heavy atmosphere of grudging concession. Unhappy, grudging concession.

"How are you getting to the airport?" Brieann asked. Now that the big decision was made, all that was left were the details.

"Uber, I guess," I said. "We have to leave before lunch. All I've got is a free period and I can't gym anyway."

"I can take you," Drew offered, still grouchy. "That'll be one less thing we'd have to worry about." He kicked the grass, annoyed with me but unable to do anything about it.

I smiled at him. His protests came from a place of love and I appreciated that just as much as I did his support.

"Where are you going to stay when you're there?" Brieann may not like this flying idea but she was still going to make sure things went as smoothly as possible.

"Liam lives just right outside the city. I figure I can call either him or Chase and stay with them." I shrugged. "And if that won't work, I can call a whole bunch of other people. There's 17 years worth of names and numbers I can fall back on."

"I'll leave my Dad a note with all the important stuff … flight numbers, itinerary … that sort of thing," I assured them. "By the time he gets home to read it, he won't be able to stop us, but he'll know where we are."

"The police won't be involved," Drew said to Brieann sarcastically. "Another thing we won't have to worry about." She frowned at him but didn't disagree. They were really hating this.

"I still think your Dad is going to be ropeable when this is all over," Ethan said but he wasn't aggressively flashing his blade, just spinning. "Your family is Sweet As. Your dad is brilliant. He knows nothing about me but welcomes me. In return, his daughter runs off with the dodgy Kiwi to the Big Smoke." He shook his head. "It's not right."

"I can go on my own," I threatened.

I didn't think he could be any more upset but his face darkened. "That's even worse," he said sharply, his eyes hard on me. He closed the blade and gripped the handle hard.

"And I'm not running away. It's Chicago, not New Zealand. It's not like I'm leaving the country. It's just the Midwest." I appealed to them again, not to win any arguments but just so that they wouldn't feel so bad. "We already have return tickets for Sunday. It's legit just the weekend. I won't even miss any school."

"Except gym." Drew was just being contrary.

"Which doesn't even count," I pointed out.

"I have such a bad feeling about this," Brieann said, holding her stomach. Drew put both hands behind his head, closed his eyes and grimaced. He felt the same.

I looked at Ethan for support. His jaw was set and his expression fierce. He caught me looking at him and his face softened. He put his knife away and tilted his head to the side, an invitation. I leaned against him. He sighed.

"On the upside," he said in surrender. "At least no one is shooting at us this time."

Tourists

It didn't help Ethan's mood that he had to leave his precious butterfly knife behind. We weren't taking any luggage and it probably wouldn't have bode well with the TSA if he tried to bring it on board. Drew, on the other hand, looked very pleased to be left in charge of it.

"Don't take that to school," I warned him through the open door of his BMW. "Don't play with it. You'll hurt yourself. Make sure you keep it safe. Or he'll kill you."

He rolled his eyes and nodded. "I know … I know … I've been thoroughly warned." He leaned across the passenger's seat. "Text me when you land."

I waved at him. "Yes, Dad."

I was teasing him, but my throat tightened with the reminder that my father was going to come home to an empty house that night. He'll find the note I left him, and he was going to be straight up pissed.

It looked like he was going to say something more but the traffic guard waved him to move forward. I slammed the door closed for him. He waved one more time; then eased back into the flow of cars.

Ethan was waiting by sliding doors of the airport entrance, his duffel slung over his good shoulder. I hefted my pack on both of my shoulders and joined him. He looked very unhappy.

"Thank you," I said to him. I told him that I could've done this alone, and that was true. I was scared but I would have still done it. Having him with me fortified my resolve. It was one thing not to feel alone. It was another to be actively strengthened by who you were with. I couldn't explain how much it meant to me that he was here.

However involuntarily.

"You're infuriatingly stubborn, you know that?" He has said this before, but he also said it with fondness.

"What does that say about you?" I teased.

He grinned, his hazel eyes twinkled. "Well, we all know how mad I am. That's no surprise."

I was still worried when we went through security. The fact that Ethan didn't think of his very dangerous knife as a weapon made me wonder if there were other weapons on him that he didn't think worth declaring. I should've at least checked his duffel before we left the house.

I don't know what it was like for him before, but Ethan looked equal parts confused and suspicious as we went through the line. If I were security, I'd have pulled him aside for a closer check just because of the way he was acting.

TSA cleared him.

I hadn't realized how much of my anxiety hinged on that. I was so relieved that I was in a much better mood while I was putting my Chucks back on.

"Let's go pick up some candy," I said, slinging my pack over one shoulder.

"I have some for you, if you want," he offered. I loved that he carried sweets with him at all times just for me.

"No, not for me. It's compensation."

I may as well have been TSA with how confused he looked.

"*See's Candies* are a California staple. You can't just find them anywhere in Chicago. They'll make for a good incentive for old friends to come help us if we need them." I shrugged. "And if we don't need them, then we have good candy."

His lips tugged to one side. "I was almost impressed until you revealed your true ulterior motive."

"We should probably grab a couple of bottles of water too, while we're at it. And something to eat. We're arriving after dinner and I'd rather not be, you know, *hangry*." I headed toward our gate, pulling him along.

We walked past two different coffee shops before finding a kiosk that carried what we needed. I handed the cashier my credit card, wondering if it was going to be declined. Considering the big purchases I've made, maybe I've hit my limit.

The transaction went through without issues. When she returned my card, I felt a renewed tug of guilt. Dad was probably going to confiscate this by the time this was all over. My savings will be depleted, and I'll have to get a steady summer job to pay back what I owe him. And then some. Not to mention the emotional damage it was going to cause on our relationship.

Still worth it, I repeated to myself. I looked up at Ethan. He was a reminder that the impossible doesn't always have to stay impossible. What would have happened if he had given up on me? What would have happened if he didn't decide to find me? He was a testament that dreams can come true if you don't let fear stop you.

It was my turn to believe.

"You're an experienced traveler," Ethan observed, as I made space for our water bottles in my pack.

I thought about all the family vacations I had growing up. My family had been lucky enough to afford annual vacations. Dad insisted. It was one of the perks of being able to take weeks off work. He always said that travel was a different kind of education. Something we couldn't learn from the classroom … or even the Internet, in all its glory.

"Flying is fun. I didn't like road trips," I admitted. "I love the idea of being able to have adventures before you even get to your destination, but I get car sick pretty quickly. Nausea has a way of ruining an experience. It's not the kind of adventure you want to remember."

The last time we had attempted a family road trip, I threw up in the car. On Locke. We turned around and spent the rest of our vacation at home. Dad sold the car later that year. Even after numerous detailing and friends assuring us that the car smelled fine, it was never the same. It was like we couldn't get the smell out of our heads. And Locke refused to sit next to me for years.

Flying never bothered me. I liked to fly.

"I was dizzy on the plane coming here," Ethan complained. "I didn't chunder but it didn't feel very good. And my ears hurt."

I don't know why but his admission made him that much more attractive. He was just so cute. Maybe it was that he could admit a weakness. Or maybe it was just nice knowing that there was something I was better at than he was.

"You're adorable," I said aloud. "I know what you're talking about but it doesn't feel as bad as being on a boat. It's like being on a roller coaster."

"I don't like roller coasters. And you're just showing off that you've been on a boat," he teased.

"I am not." Maybe I was but I didn't want to admit it after he had caught me. "But wait, you like fast but you don't like coasters? Why? Is it the height thing?" I could understand that. I didn't like heights, but planes didn't feel that way. Maybe you were so high up that it didn't feel like you were high up.

"It's that feeling I hate." He put a hand on his stomach. "Not nausea. More like queasy."

"Isn't nausea and queasy the same exact thing?"

"Less chunder and more just dodgy."

I laughed. "I literally don't know what you just said."

It felt good to laugh. Genuinely. This whole venture felt like someone had poured melted Popsicle juice over my entire world. Everything I was doing felt sticky and gross. Laughing with Ethan about barf would've been the last thing I'd have thought would cut through the grunge, but it did.

"Gum helps with the pressure in your ears." I couldn't do anything about his dodgy chunder. But I could solve one of his problems.

"Gum? Oh, like chuddy? What am I supposed to do? Stuff it in my ears?" He was smiling at me so I knew he didn't mean it. He was allowing this small intermission before we would, eventually, have to face a more serious situation.

"Yes," I said, calling his bluff. "You need a whole lot of … chuddy. Once you stick it in your ears, you won't hear the air pressure coming." I didn't even bother to try to keep a straight face. "That's why you always see us Americans chewing gum. We're protecting our brains."

He pretended to take me seriously, rubbing his chin in exaggerated concentration. "Yes, yes, I see that. Very scientific. Makes total sense."

I was still laughing at his bad acting when he leaned forward so that our foreheads were touching. He lowered his voice and foolishness melted into sincerity with each word. "You. Are. So. Smart."

I felt heat on my face. I was glad that he was too close to see. He kissed me. "I'm so lucky to have found you."

When he pulled away, his expression was no longer playful. The gold and green in his eyes were perfectly balanced. He wasn't anxious or unhappy anymore. With a renewed sense of determination he promised, "London, I love you. I will follow you anywhere."

Inflight Entertainment

I had to stop myself from texting Dad before boarding. I was so used to letting him know where I was and what I was doing. It added to my overall anxiety. I was doing something wrong by breaking my established routine.

He'd know everything when he got home. That would have to do. I texted Drew and Brieann instead.

"Did you fly here in first class?" I asked Ethan. His flight to the US was sponsored by actual royalty; so I would assume that he received the best of the best.

"I don't know what that means," he said, stuffing his duffel under the seat in front of him. A shadow of annoyance fell over his face. "But I did have more room than this."

"At least this isn't an 18-hour flight." How unfortunate that his indoctrination to flying was such a long haul. "Easy peasy."

I let him sit by the window, arguing that it minimized the chances of someone bumping into his bad arm. He resisted at first, but I felt that he secretly wanted it. I understood that. I loved being next to the window but between the two of us, I think I've logged my fair share of that experience. He deserved this joy.

"What did you do for 18 hours?" I asked.

"I slept a lot." He lifted his right elbow. "I was at the tail end of some pretty strong painkillers; so it was easy to sleep." He looked around with a frown. "I also had a pillow and a blanket then."

I grinned. "You're so spoiled."

Sleep did sound like a good idea. I had been so wired but from experience, I knew that the hum of the engines and the recycled cabin air would make me sleepy once we were on our way. I pulled off my thick hoodie and rolled it up into a ball. "Ta-da, a pillow!" I offered it to him but he didn't take it.

"Are you going to try *skipping*?" He was trying to be nonchalant but I could hear the concern in his voice.

"It's sometimes unnerving that you can read me so well," I mumbled. "Honestly, I don't know how."

I had tried last night to no avail. It would have been nice to get some feedback. Maybe an assurance of some kind that we were on the right track. "I want to," I admitted, knowing that wasn't what he wanted to hear.

He gave me a sharp nod. "It sounds dodgy to me but did you try that chocka yoga stuff that Brieann suggested?"

"Are you trying to help me?" I was expecting him to try and talk me out of it. He had made it abundantly clear how he felt about dream *skipping*. It was contrary to all his arguments that he was encouraging me to use it now.

He looked very annoyed. "I'm here, aren't I? Of course I'm trying to help you. That's always been the objective."

I felt bad. He had made so many sacrifices and instead of gratitude, I was questioning his motivations.

"I'm sorry. That's not what I meant," I said immediately. "I know you don't approve of it. It just caught me by surprise."

He sighed. He rubbed two fingers on his forehead as if to erase a headache that just manifested itself. "I think," he said, still massaging his temples, "that knowing how to control it should probably be your first priority."

He dropped his hand and looked straight at me, his face very serious. It was unfair that he could look just as attractive when he smiled as he did deadpanned. It was almost distracting.

"This talent of yours … think of it like my knife."

"This isn't a weapon," I argued. He closed his eyes at my interruption so I stopped. I was being rude. I gave him an apologetic look, and he accepted it by continuing as though I hadn't attacked him.

"This power can be just as dangerous if you don't know how to handle it properly. It can hurt you or it can hurt others. Imagine if I just decided to toss my knife around without first learning how to use it. How much damage would that cause?" I could see now why he used his knife as an analogy. He was right, of course. There were consequences to everything.

"You don't even know what you are really capable of," he continued gently. "And you don't know what it will cost you."

I nodded somberly to show him that I was listening, not arguing. His concerns were valid.

"The safest thing, in my opinion, is to leave it alone. Just like if I didn't want to risk getting cut, the best thing would be to avoid the knife all together."

"But you still mess with your knife, regardless of the danger," I pointed out.

"Yes, but I've also learned how to control it. And that knowledge didn't come without blood payments." I remembered how easily he was cut by the unforgiving blade that one time we were together. A slight distraction was all it took, and we were lucky it wasn't worse.

"I understand why it's important to you. Truly, I do. Some things are worth it," he agreed. "I think using it because you don't want to use the phone is frivolous and unnecessary." He let the sentence hang in the air, testing my response. I pouted but didn't disagree. "But your mother is, without a doubt, a deserving cause."

He was so much more mature than I was. I couldn't appreciate him more.

"Thank you." It sounded so flimsy. I didn't have the ability to put into words how incredible he was as a human being. How grateful I was that he chose to be with me. "I love you." Better, but still not enough. "I really, really love you." I was just so bad at this. I pleaded with the world that he would understand everything I was trying to say.

He took my hand and brought it to his lips, giving it a tender kiss. "I love you, too."

It made a difference, knowing that he was here because he believed in what I was doing and not just because I forced him to come. I felt my hope expand, bringing with it renewed energy.

"OK, so Bree talked about focus on centering." I shifted in my seat so that I had both hands on the arm rests, my back straight and my toes just touching the carpeted floor. "Deep breaths." I took a deep breath, filling my lungs. I held it as long as I could before slowly releasing it, mentally counting the seconds. Ethan hadn't moved, unwilling to disturb me.

I repeated the process a few times, becoming more aware of my immediate surroundings. It was easy to tune out the flight attendants going through their perfunctory safety demonstration.

I paid attention to them as often as I would read the Terms And Conditions of every app I've ever downloaded. Which is to say never. I barely registered other passengers shifting in their seats. I felt the plane jerk forward on the runway but it didn't provoke a reaction from me.

I was imagining a bubble around me that was getting smaller. It blocked out everything around it, but it amplified everything within.

A stray hair was brushing on my cheek that had to be pulled back into place. My neck was stiff. I had to roll my head a few times before I could continue. The longer I did this, the more minute things bothered me. My jeans felt restrictive. My socks were uneven. I swear that I could feel the actual outline of the life vest underneath my seat. These little things were louder and more distracting than the plane's engine when we finally took flight.

I imagined the bubble tighter around me until I was paying more attention to my heartbeat. I could imagine the air filling my lungs, taking the oxygen I needed and expelling the rest. I could almost hear my blood flowing in my veins. My pulse was like a bass drum, setting the rhythm for the rest of my body.

I didn't know what my swirling wheels of energy might look like. Maybe like a mini hurricane from space? Maybe a tornado? Either analogy felt too chaotic. Without realizing I had made a conscious decision. I imagined the pulsing of a bright star. Like the ones that were above us when Ethan and I had kissed. Seemingly far away but also filled with promise.

The stars in my mind brightened, filling the space with nothing but white light.

And when it faded, I found myself alone on solid ground. 2,000 miles away from where I started.

Flicker

It worked.

The snow on the ground wasn't as thick as before but it was there, disturbed by vehicles and footsteps that threaded through this back alley. It was still cold. For whatever reason, when I *skipped*, I had left my hoodie behind.

I had at least been smart enough to wear a long-sleeved shirt. I tugged the sleeves as far as they would go over my exposed wrists. The sun was hidden behind clouds, casting everything in a bluish tone.

"Mom?" I called. I heard the urgency in my voice. "Are you here?"

I was more careful making my way to the shelter, knowing that another clumsy fall would cause more damage at such a critical point. I could not afford that kind of stupid mistake. I didn't see her at first. That awful feeling of trepidation started in my stomach. What if everyone was right? What if she wasn't even here?

The shawl looked brighter under the blue toned light. I saw it first. As I got closer, I could tell that something was wrong. I had noticed it before but it seemed so much stronger now.

She flickered. Just her and not anything else around her. It was like watching an old film. She was solid and then she was not. I blinked a few times, unconsciously trying to align my sight with seconds when she was fixed.

She didn't turn to look at me. The shawl was a ball in her arms and she was curled around it. A crumpled version of herself. A ball over another ball. That was how she looked.

Things weren't as intimidating as they had been. Maybe it was the sun, shielded as it was. Maybe it was because the surroundings were less forbidding now that I've recognized them. Maybe it was because I was convinced of what I was seeing. Of *whom* I was seeing.

I reached out to her, and my hand landed on her shoulder. Even though her image seemed to flicker, her tangibility was fixed. She was glacial to the touch but she remained substantial. A slight movement was the only indication that she noticed my touch. She did not move her head.

"It's too cold," she mumbled between shivers. "Can't leave."

It didn't make sense that she didn't put the shawl over herself but it also wasn't as cold as she made it seem. Yes, I would have been much more comfortable in a hoodie, but even with just one layer on, I was cold but nowhere near frostbite.

As if to confuse me more, the clouds gave way to the sun, almost instantly warming the atmosphere with yellow light. I looked up at it and felt the difference on my face. My mother gave no indication that there was any kind of change.

I knelt next to her. She was rocking gently back and forth. "Help," she whimpered to no one in particular. "Please, please …"

"Mom?" I tried again. "Hold on, OK?" She continued rocking, as if unaware of my presence. Or that my presence didn't matter.

I felt an urgency that I didn't before. A sense that time was running out. Ethan and I may be too late.

I hated to leave her, but if I can get someone here to help her now, that may make the difference. "I'm going to find help, OK?"

Something got through to her and she looked up at me. "Help?"

"Yes, Mom," I said, encouraged by her response.

"Will you help me? Please?"

"Yes, yes, of course," I said, exaggerating my response with movements, trying to keep her attention.

"I ... I can't see you very well ..."

Maybe she saw me the same way I saw her. Flickering. That was never true with Ethan. Was it because of how I got here? I didn't understand.

"I don't know," I said. "I'm here but ... I'm not here ... yet ..." Her eyes glazed over, bewildered. That was probably the stupidest response I could have said to someone already as confused as she was. I cursed silently at the wasted opportunity.

"It doesn't matter," I pivoted. "I'll get help. Get you out of this cold." She didn't respond. I had lost her again. "Mom?"

I was wasting time trying to get through to her when I could be getting her to someplace warm. Or at least find her better coverage against the cold if she refused to leave. I bit my lip, silently promising that I'd return. I had every intention of finding a solution for her but when I stood up, she said my name.

"London," she whispered.

I froze, unable to think or move. I wasn't even breathing. I was afraid that anything I did might dispel the very delicate cloud of her consciousness.

She reached for my arm and I braced myself to feel the coldness of her touch, as I had before. I felt a different sensation. I knew I had run out of time.

Artie

My eyes flew open, and I saw the dull gray plastic of the airline seat in front of me. I hadn't realized I had been holding my breath until I gasped aloud.

I felt a warm hand over my wrist and even before I turned, I knew it would be Ethan. I knew that I was back on a plane, thousands of miles in the air, probably somewhere over Utah. I closed my eyes tightly in frustration. The only thing that stopped me from shouting the vile curse I was loudly thinking was the presence of the innocent toddler sitting across the aisle from us.

"It worked," Ethan said as a statement of fact.

I nodded, still not ready to talk. My frustration and anger were not quite under control yet.

"I could almost tell exactly when it happened," he said in a hushed voice. "You were so still. Your breathing was shallow. It was like a trance."

That sounded like a significant improvement over having a seizure, like the first time I met Ethan. I didn't have a migraine this time either. Other than the emotional impact, all I felt was stiffness in my joints.

"I saw her," I finally said, matching the volume of his voice. "She said my name."

"So we're good?" Ethan asked, knowing that we weren't but also not knowing exactly why.

"No." I knew he wasn't surprised to hear that. "I couldn't tell if it was this Chicago or alternate universe Chicago or even spirit world Chicago." I felt the tears in my eyes before I realized that I was upset enough to cry.

"She was … flickering." I hated to admit it. Admitting it aloud gave it permission to be real. "Like a bad film. And she said she couldn't see me very well either. It was weird." The optimism I had been holding melted into a dense feeling of dread settling in the pit of my stomach.

"Yeah, that doesn't sound right," Ethan agreed reluctantly. "Anytime you *skipped* to me, there was nothing to say that you weren't anything but real." He confirmed what I already knew was true.

"I don't know what's wrong." I wiped my eyes with the back of my sleeve. Crying made me feel weaker and more helpless. Which also made me angrier. Ethan reached around me to pull me toward him until our foreheads touched.

"This is progress," he reminded me. "Give yourself a break. You can't expect to master your abilities on the first try."

Yes, this was progress. It just didn't feel like it. Instead, it felt like even more obstacles awaited.

"I feel like I'm going backward." It didn't make sense but, then again, feelings don't always make sense.

"You're attempting to control something we can't fully explain. You don't have the benefit of a guide, a teacher, or even a textbook. This is trial and error for a science that hasn't been named yet." He was putting facts in perspective so my emotions could catch up.

"Clarke's Second Law," I said, nodding.

He paused in the middle of what he was about to say, knitted his eyebrows together, and tilted his head to the side. I smiled at his confusion.

"Clarke's Second Law," I repeated as if that would clarify things.

He shook his head. "You can say it as often as you want. I still won't know what you're talking about."

I smiled bigger. "Sir Arthur C Clarke. Sci-fi master. He had three … or was it four? Maybe it was four?" I looked to Ethan for help. He shook his head again, still confused but now equally amused. "Nevermind," I amended. "He had these laws he made up based on observations regarding the nature of technology and discovery."

"I wager you know what these laws are," he said, suppressing a smile.

"I know the second one," I said with any certainty. "And the third." I was worried that I wouldn't be able to quote the others as well.

"Let's hear that second law then," he said, giving me a platform for my Sci-Fi geek moment to shine.

"The only way of discovering the limits of the possible is to venture a little way past them into the impossible." I quoted with ill-concealed pride.

Ethan smiled. "Well, if Artie says that, then you know it's true."

I felt better already. Ethan had talents that went far beyond how well he flipped a knife.

"You've already done the impossible," he said. "Wherever you venture now is already past that."

The L

I tried again during the flight but I couldn't recreate my previous success. Maybe because when I first tried it, I wasn't really expecting to make any progress. After that, expectations were high and so was my adrenaline. Then in the middle of my attempt, I actually fell asleep.

I woke up when the pilot announced that we were approaching descent. I failed.

"She'll be 'right," Ethan said gently. "You don't need to skip. We're here." I hadn't said anything but he must've still noticed my agitation.

"Oh! Gum!" I had put it in one of the outside pockets of my pack for easy access. "Here." I handed him a cube. "Chew some chuddy. And swallow a lot."

"Swallow the chuddy?"

"No, no, not the gum. Just … swallow nothing. It helps equalize the pressure in your ears. Or yawn. I like to yawn a lot."

His smile was just a slight tugging on his lips but his swallowing was exaggerated to show me he was following my advice. I made yawning motions to encourage him. He snorted a laugh but followed suit with unconvincing overemphasis.

"It helps!" I insisted.

"Oh, you're helping plenty already," he assured me playfully, punctuating his words with another dramatic yawn.

Despite his doubts and theatrics, my suggestions did work. He conceded as much when we landed. I considered the achievement to be a good sign for what was to come.

My phone wouldn't stop beeping when I finally turned it back on. I was reading multiple text messages from both Brieann and Drew when the plane doors were opened.

Dad left voicemails. I wasn't ready to hear them yet.

"Are we in the city?" Ethan asked. We didn't need to stop at baggage claim so we could bypass it. I had my pack over one shoulder and my phone on my other hand, still scrolling through messages and bracing myself to listen to Dad's voicemail.

I zipped up my thick hoodie in anticipation for the cold. "Sort of? Not near enough to where we need to be." I was thinking aloud. "But we can take the L straight there."

"The … L?"

"The train," I clarified.

He considered my answer for a moment then nodded in understanding. "Ah. Is the rail shaped that way then?"

Now, I was confused. "Shaped what way?"

"An L?" he asked. "Is that why they call it an L?"

I laughed. "No, no. It's called the L because it's short for "elevated"."

He was incredulous. "You do know that "elevated" begins with the letter E, yeah?"

"Yes, but it sounds like the letter L," I argued weakly.

"Is this a London thing?" he asked suspiciously. "Because all things London, so it has to be an L?"

"No, seriously!" I was suddenly very defensive. "I'm not the only one that calls it the L."

"You're telling me that it's an American thing?"

"Well, no, not an American thing," I admitted. Not everyone knew it was called the L. It was more of a local Chicago quirk.

"So, you're making it up," he accused before I could explain.

"I swear it's officially called the L," I was laughing because of how silly the conversation was and how weak my arguments sounded. It did nothing for my credibility.

"Uh huh," he said, eyebrows raised and completely unconvinced.

"Come on," I said. "We can ask the attendant and they'll tell you." I was leading the way to the transit exit. O'Hare International Airport used to be the busiest airport in the country when I was growing up. While that designation has since been taken away, you wouldn't know by how many people we were bumping into. It still remained bustling and crowded.

My phone rang. I winced, anticipating the dreaded call from Dad. I looked at Ethan for suggestions. He was serious but he didn't say anything. I considered rejecting the call.

It wasn't Dad calling, but Liam. It may as well have been Dad calling, but I answered it anyway.

"I'm outside the Terminal 2 exit waiting for you," he said, his voice clipped. He waited for me to acknowledge that and then hung up.

I suppose I could have just ignored him. Ethan and I could have just taken the train while Liam circled the parking lot indefinitely. I was already in massive trouble, I may as well have gone at it full force.

Instead, I felt like a toddler caught trying to take a candy bar from the grocery store checkout line. I was caught before I could take a bite. Adults with disapproving looks were surrounding me with their hands on their hips. I had to 'fess up.

I was holding back tears when I looked at Ethan. "Looks like there's a different L waiting for us."

Consequences

The ride back to Liam's apartment was not pleasant.

I had finally gotten the nerve to listen to the voicemails that Dad left. He was livid. His after-school meeting was canceled so that he got to the letter I left him a little earlier than I had anticipated.

The first call was the ineffectual but expected call of an angry father that served no purpose other than to express disapproval.

The second, a few minutes later, was calmer, though no less furious. He had called Liam to come get us. And in a maneuver that was fueled more by wrath than logic, he booked a flight for himself to follow us.

I suppose he'd rather yell at me while he was at the peak of his outrage rather than wait a few days and risk calming down.

It did not look good.

"And thanks to you," Liam was saying, "I have to make the wonderful trip back to this traffic hell hole at four in the effing morning to get him." He accelerated a little too aggressively into the next lane just to emphasize his dissatisfaction.

Taking the Red Eye trip was not going to help mollify the situation. I wondered if Dad did that on purpose.

"So stupid."

I couldn't explain to him why; so I didn't say much of anything and let him think whatever he was thinking. Ethan wasn't contributing either. He knew enough to identify a hostile situation. Maybe he was secretly relieved we were now back in family custody.

We were almost at Liam's apartment before he grudgingly pulled into a drive through. As angry as he was, his programming wouldn't let us starve. Since I had been on a steady diet of anxiety, I didn't think I'd have much of an appetite. The extra large fries I ordered on top of the regular value meal determined that was a lie.

"Don't eat that in the car," Liam warned. Ordinarily, I would've defied him to sneak a fry or two but this didn't seem like an appropriate time to antagonize him. I kept the bag on my lap. The patented smell of deep fried genetically modified starch wafted through the paper, triggering the deep desire for the comfort one can only find in food that is certifiably unhealthy.

I was able to resist and meekly followed my brother into his building. He wasn't completely done berating me, but it was getting late. Knowing he had to be up again in a few hours had derailed his momentum.

"Take the couch," he ordered Ethan. "There's a futon in the other room," he said to me, pointing to the first door down a very tight hallway. "There might be stuff in the closet, I don't know. Figure it out."

He grabbed a drink for himself, leaning back against the kitchen counter to address us. "This isn't a prom after-party so keep your hands to yourselves and stay in separate rooms."

I knew I was blushing because I could feel the mortification manifesting itself physically. I couldn't even look at Ethan. His presumptions were so unfair.

I also knew that I didn't have the ground to stand on. That was exactly why he was doing it. It was a reminder of all the trouble I was in without having to state the obvious repeatedly. This was just one of his creative and effective methods of getting his point across. He had honed his technique over years of being the eldest.

He waited a beat. Years of being the youngest taught me that it was an opening I knew I shouldn't take. I fumed in silence. Unsatisfied with my lack of response, he gave up. "I'm going to bed before this day gets any worse," he announced unnecessarily, making the dramatic exit to his room.

I closed my eyes and exhaled only when I heard his door close. The tension had followed my brother out. When I looked at Ethan, his expression wasn't one of accusation. He had every right to a justified I-Told-You-So but instead, he was concerned. Seeing that level of acceptance in his eyes filled mine with tears.

I let the fries get cold in the bag. I hugged Ethan and wept. He held me, allowing me to empty the paradoxical emotions that I was under-equipped to process properly.

"She'll be 'right, London," he whispered in my hair over and over again until I believed him.

Jailbreak

I didn't bother unfolding the futon. I didn't even bother looking in the closet as Liam suggested. Neither would have improved the circumstances.

I did shower and brush my teeth. It helped wash away the muck I usually associated with travel. Not to mention the emotional heaviness I was carrying. A shower helped erase evidence of tears.

I didn't sleep much, and I was too worked up to successfully *dream skip*. For the most part, I just stared into the darkness until my eyes were acclimated enough to identify the odd items that were stored in the room out of necessity rather than aesthetic. The more time passed, the more alert I was, listening for when Liam leaves.

This room had belonged to Chase before he decided to move out on his own last year. He and Liam had shared this apartment for almost four years. It was a big change for them both but not so much for me. Last year, I was still living in the same house that I grew up in. Same school. Same sets of friends.

When Liam went to college years ago, I wasn't even 10 yet. Adjusting to his visits was easy. I was young enough to have been so self-involved to even have noticed much of a change.

It was a little different when Chase graduated high school. I was actively involved in the pomp and circumstance. I helped organize his graduation party. But Chase often kept to himself; so his actual absence, when the time came, wasn't a massive variance to me.

Locke heading to college was really the first big change.

I had spent the most time with him when I was growing up, following him around like the stereotypical little sister that he couldn't ditch. Except that Locke didn't mind so much. I suspected that he enjoyed flexing his big brother authority over me in the same way that Liam did over all of us.

It was beneficial to me, too. I was in with the cool crowd without any effort on my part. His friends looked out for me, which I suppose also contributed to my lack of desire to find my own real friends.

He left for college last year and for the first time in my life, without my older brothers dictating terms, I was alone to do what I really wanted. For the first time, I was *discovering* what I really wanted.

I discovered that I didn't really like Oreos as much as I thought I did. Chewy Chocolate Chip cookies were more my speed. I drank more water instead of pop. I spent more time drawing. I was at the library more often. I stopped binge watching shows that I actually didn't care about. In fact, the screen was often dark until Dad came home. Little by little, I found that I had my own personality.

Then we moved.

They say that moving is among the three most stressful events in life. Right up there with losing a loved one to death.

It was Dad's idea. He thought he had to work to sell me the proposition; so he pitched it with an over-enthusiastic, premeditated spiel worthy of an As-seen-on-TV. I thought it was a welcome change. I had just started to get to know myself; so the move gave me an excuse to start over.

In hindsight, the spiel might have been largely for his own benefit. He had more reservations about the move than he would admit. Change was always difficult and he's had it come at him from every angle lately. He's had to pivot and adjust so many times. Was there any room left for him to maneuver?

I felt the guilt. I knew that plenty might have been avoided had I not been so selfish. That's what was behind Liam's anger. He could see how hard it's been on Dad, and he had expected me to ease the strain, not to add to it.

Yet, there I was, listening for my next opportunity that would inevitably lead to more chaos. The guilt wasn't enough to stop me.

I heard the front door open and then clicked closed. I counted slowly to 20 before moving, just in case he decided to come back, but it was quiet. I checked the window that looked over the parking lot, hoping the view would provide a clue that he had left. It was facing the wrong side of the building and didn't help much. I listened for a car starting but it was impossible to tell if the faint engine sounds belonged to him or other residents of the complex.

I counted again. This time to a hundred, giving myself one more chance to change my mind. I interpreted the silence as an endorsement from the universe.

Crying always left my head feeling like it was filled with used Kleenex but the adrenaline I was experiencing after Liam's departure cleared it up. I pulled my phone off its charger, threw on my hoodie, and grabbed my pack.

I was convinced that Liam had left the building but I opened the bedroom door slowly anyway, in case I had been wrong. Down the hall, Liam's door was ajar, further evidence that he had gone. I found Ethan lying on the couch.

It occurred to me that I'd never seen him asleep before. It was sufficient to make me stop and appreciate this intermission.

He was on his side, curled up to be able to fit on the cramped accommodations. He had one arm tucked under his head and the other, out of its customary sling, was slightly dangling off the edge. His gray undershirt was pulled tight over his boot-camp defined shoulders. His breathing was steady and he made a deep ocean sound through his nose whenever he exhaled. The flood light outside the sliding door, partially blocked by the blinds, cast striped shadows over him. He must have been exhausted, as deeply asleep as he was. Just the same, he looked peaceful. Untroubled.

This might have been the one thing that would stop me, my unwillingness to wake him.

Whether I wasn't as quiet as I thought I was or if it was years of living on the streets, something alerted him that he wasn't alone. He didn't immediately open his eyes but I knew he was awake because I saw the tensing in his muscles and the change in his breathing. Just as regular but also deliberately measured.

"Ethan?" I whispered so that he knew that he didn't have to pretend. He opened his eyes.

"Your brother just left," he told me, proving that he wasn't as unconscious of his environment as he appeared.

I nodded. "Yes, I know. Let's go." I rummaged through the bowl Liam left by the front door. I didn't find an extra set of keys to the apartment but I did find his CTA pass. I didn't know if it was loaded but anything helped. I pocketed it.

Ethan swung his legs off the couch and immediately started to put his boots on. "We're leaving?" he asked without stopping.

"If we leave now, we can catch the 4:45 a.m. train," I responded. Inspired by my find, I was randomly opening drawers to see if there was anything else we may be able to use. I had cash but anything to add to that wouldn't hurt. "I doubt my credit card will work now. I'll text them when we get downtown, so they'll know where we are."

He was ready to go by the time I turned around. He didn't look like he agreed with my plan. His eyebrows were pinched together and his expression severe. His willingness to support me before his questions were answered was a testament to how much he trusted me. I may never be worthy of that level of faith.

I closed the distance between us so that I could touch him when I spoke. It always felt better to be able to connect with him physically when we were talking about things we might not agree on. Our tactile tether to each other was a reminder of what was really important. It was not about who wins an argument. It was about finding the solution together.

"We have this last chance, Ethan," I pleaded. "We've come this far. I don't want it to be for nothing. At the very least, we should find out."

His jaw tightened. I didn't know if that was progress or if he was preparing to disagree. I didn't want to waste much more time on this. Missing the train would cost dearly. I had to push with everything I had.

"I'm not asking you to let me go on a suicide mission with very little hope of survival here." It was a reminder of what he had asked from me just a month ago. The stakes were higher then, of course, but at its most basic level, I was asking for the same thing.

"That's not fair," he complained. He had been right at the time. It had been the best course and everything turned out in the end. It didn't change the sacrifices or the damage that had been done. It was just worth it.

"No, it's not," I agreed. "This is much less dangerous."

I raised my eyebrows in response to his sardonic expression, daring him to argue with that. He didn't say anything.

"At least no one is shooting at us this time?" I quoted him, phrasing it like a question. "Right?"

His expression was softened by that half-smile I loved. He pulled me into a tight hug, his way of consenting to a plan he otherwise disliked. When I pulled away, a new expression had replaced the sarcasm.

I'd seen it before. It was the soldier in him. It was the man that he decided he wanted to be. It was a look of determination that was unstoppable even by the impossible. It canceled all my doubts.

We were going to complete this mission.

Refuge

"This is our stop," I told Ethan. I was checking the digital clock on my phone, trying to figure out how much time we had left. Dad's flight was arriving in roughly 10 minutes. If all went smoothly for them, that gave us a little less than an hour before he and Liam discovered that we were gone. I wanted to reach them before that happened. Waiting too long would only make things worse.

I had to stand on the platform a couple of minutes even after the train had left, just so I could get my bearings. I hadn't ridden on the L for almost six months, and not ever this early in the morning. It felt so foreign to me. I could have easily mistaken this for the dream.

I had left Liam's apartment with strong optimism. That must've gotten off on an earlier platform because I didn't feel it now. I was struggling with an adverse volley of self doubt.

A cold wind gust reminded me that we might already be too late. I felt the pressure of the looming deadlines. My internal existential crisis can wait. My mother cannot.

We would have run most of the way, but the sidewalks hadn't all been completely cleared of the snow. After almost wiping out on ice, I had to slow down. My ankle was reminding me how easily this whole endeavor can come to an end by one bad landing. We paced ourselves. We did a jog on drier pavement and walked through areas that hadn't been salted or exposed to enough light.

It helped that the morning rush hadn't yet begun. The holiday season promised that weekends in the city would be just as crazy as a regular workday, if not more. We passed tents that were already erected in empty plazas, getting ready for weekend festivities. Faint Christmas music wafted from stores that were not yet open. It was still dark. All the streetlights were on.

My heart pounded louder the farther we got. A thin trickle of sweat ran down the back of my neck. We weaved through obstacles ranging from stacked outdoor furniture to heavy piles of dirty snow from city plows. City blocks never seemed so big to me as they did then.

My throat was dry. I had a bottle of water in my pack but I didn't want to stop. Ethan didn't look like he was being physically challenged at all despite having had recent surgery. I envied that.

We had made it to the wide bridge that I was using as my landmark. I stopped at the corner and did a slow wide turn to confirm. This had to be the spot. Down to the bright red awning and potted evergreens. Exactly how I last saw it.

I didn't have to tell Ethan. He jerked his chin, a quick nod, the moment we made eye contact. The momentary success must have been all over my face.

We turned down the alley where my Mom should be waiting. When we passed the same cars parked on the street, still covered with snow, it further confirmed that we were heading the right way. My heart raced. My breath, loud and haggard, was all I could hear. It was louder than the cars down the main street. Louder than our footsteps in the snow.

I saw her shawl.

That should have made me run. That should have made me rush forward in an effort to get to her faster. We were racing against time and the elements. Finding her was the whole point. Finding her validated everything.

But when I saw this, when I saw I was right to do this, I did the opposite.

I froze.

Ethan almost ran into me. He stopped when I did and followed my stare to the shelter. When I didn't move, he dropped his duffel to the snow-covered ground and slowly walked the rest of the way. I let him go, still unable to move. Unable to even breathe.

I should have been the one leading the way, knowing what to find. Instead, I watched Ethan's careful approach. He knelt next to the figure under the shawl and lay a gentle hand on her. He looked sharply at me and then back down at her, not saying anything to betray the astonishment that was clear on his face.

I didn't blink but the world shimmered. It flickered like someone was strobing lights in my head. My worlds collided all at once. My dream world and the real world made a Venn diagram being forced to overlap to form one circle. My dream world was being made to fit into the other, resisting the laws of physics. They scraped together like unheard metal knives across plates. I felt unstable. The ground was shaking just under my feet, and no one else's.

It was different when Ethan had come to me. It was like he was added to my reality, plucked from the best parts of my dreams. This was a grinding impact that I couldn't make any sense of.

My phone rang.

The penetrating sound anchored me back to the present. I answered it without thinking. Dad's strangled voice was a mixture of justified parental anger, concern, incredulity, and relief. I didn't even hear the words, just his voice.

"We found her," I interrupted, almost in a whisper.

Dad stopped talking.

I watched Ethan remove his jacket to drape over the seemingly useless shawl. The gesture mattered even though the extra layer may not. He had wrapped his arm around her, unafraid. The world had stopped flickering, but she had not. She could not find her place.

Ethan shook his head a few times, as if trying to clear the image he was seeing. When it did not help, he looked back at me, baffled and helpless.

"We found Mom."

Synthesis

I was provoked into action by the phone call. Dad couldn't understand what I was saying because I didn't understand it myself. Liam took the phone from him and I gave him directions to find us, using the same landmarks I did. Then Ethan, still without a jacket, left to wait for them at the corner of the main road, under the red awning. It would be easier to spot them from there.

I was alone with my mother.

I pulled Ethan's jacket tighter around her, trying to hold her to the present, trying to still the flickering. Ethan was my magic; so maybe his jacket was magical too. Maybe that could mean some magic can transfer to her. It was ludicrous, of course. The wishful thinking of a desperate child. I did it anyway. As expected, it didn't make much of a difference. This was the real world.

"Mom," I tried again as I had before. This time, I wasn't worried about waking up. I was more worried that she'd disappear. The flickering had gotten worse. It was directly proportional to the rising anxiety I was feeling, fueled by the accelerating impression that we were running out of time.

Would she flicker too fast until she was completely gone? Will Ethan's jacket suddenly fall empty to the pavement?

There was no way I could begin to predict possible outcomes. This wasn't just beyond my limited experience as a human being. This was beyond logic. Without any points of comparison, how could I anticipate anything?

I didn't doubt that she was my mother, but I had no idea what she was.

She didn't acknowledge my presence any more than she had noticed Ethan's. In my dreams, she would at least see me. Here, she was on a different plane. She was the one piece of my dream world that would not properly sync into this one.

Five minutes ago, I was hoping that Dad's flight was delayed or that they would hit some traffic or that they'd just take their sweet time. Now, they couldn't get here fast enough. Dad needed to see her for himself or he'd never believe me.

I didn't believe me.

"Hold on, OK? Just hold on." I pleaded aloud more for my sake. No matter how tightly I held Ethan's jacket around her, it looked like she was getting colder. Her bottom lip trembled now and her eyes remained glassy and unfocused.

"Dad is coming," I promised, as if it would be worth anything to her. I didn't know if that would help her at all. It would make a difference to me, certainly, so I didn't sound like a lunatic. Seeing her would justify my recent actions and I may just get out of this without punishment.

That all didn't seem to matter anymore though. It was detached and unimportant. A paradigm shift was developing right in front of me. I had neither the knowledge nor the wisdom to recognize what it was in its entirety. I was positively convinced that this was crucial even though I didn't know why. Whatever it was, however it was happening, or why it was happening escaped me. One of the only things I did know was that it was happening now.

I couldn't tell how long I was sitting there with her. My phone was in my back pocket but I didn't want to let her go just to check. I had been sweating in my thick hoodie when we arrived. The sweat had long since cooled. That was my first sign of actual passing time.

I looked toward the street, hoping to see a glimpse of Ethan, Dad, or Liam. It was empty but the first hint of morning light was brightening the area. Still heavy with night, the fresh light, however slow and small, made it easier to see. I could hear the first faint sounds of a city waking in the distance. It was almost morning.

I stared at her, holding her to this world by sheer force of will, if I could. It amazed me how I had first thought of her as frightening. The lack of body hair had made her strange in the beginning. But looking at her, all I could see was beauty. She had an inner grace that was suddenly evident to me. Though her eyes were unfocused, they were still striking. There was a vibrance to her that had been worn away. When I looked more closely, I could see a residue of what was once a spirited woman.

I imagined her as the mother she could have been to me.

I never knew what I was missing. I never knew what kind of influence she would have had on me. I couldn't dream of a childhood where I would have been more supported. My family was incredible and complete. I couldn't imagine that I was lacking anything.

Maybe it wasn't that anything was insufficient but that it could have been improved. Would she have taught me the mystery behind her elusive cooking techniques? Would I be wearing more skirts instead of jeans? Would she introduce me to the secret world of female discussions that seem to intimidate the XY chromosomes in our household?

Would she be able to tell me how I was able to find Ethan? How I was able to find her?

Dad had said that she had done the same. That when she was my age, she had skipped in her sleep and met him a year before they met for real. I had inherited this baffling ability. It manifested in me the same way it did for her. It was one of the reasons he so easily welcomed Ethan. He accepted it although he couldn't explain it.

Could she?

I had been staring at her, lost in my questions of what might have been that I didn't hear the sound of hasty movements in the snow. I only looked up when I heard Dad yell my name.

Reunited

Dad never called me by my name. I was always "sweetheart" for as long as I could remember. When I was in preschool, I thought my full name was London Sweetheart Anne Evans. I didn't believe my teacher when she told me that wasn't the case. It had to be resolved over a formal parent-teacher conference after school. I had been embarrassed. Dad had been entertained.

On the way home, he explained that he would call me that so I'd never forget that I was someone special and that I was loved. I was too young to understand how meaningful that was. I was busy brooding over the embarrassment. I had pouted and refused to look at him. He took me to the store and bought me an ice cream cone. I decided it wasn't that big of a deal and accepted the bribe.

The rest of the world can call me London. Dad had his own set of rules.

I instinctively looked up when I heard my name, even though it sounded odd that it was in Dad's voice. Dad stopped where he was, not far from where I had.

She had looked up too, at the sound of my name, and had locked eyes with him. Words become superfluous. I didn't need him to confirm what I already knew.

He saw her. He knew her.

There was astonished recognition, displacing any anger that he had come armed with. His eyes widened and his jaw slackened. Anything he had meant to say after calling my name ended in a strangled cry.

Time first had been too fast and then too slow. That moment, time stopped.

I could almost see the snow by their feet suspended in the air. They were little sparkling crystals caught in the middle, reflecting the beginning of the dawn light on one side and the artificial spread of streetlights on the other.

A line had been drawn between everything we had known before and everything we were about to discover.

I was acutely aware of the wet patches on my jeans, cold against my legs. I felt the bits of snow that had melted in my shoes, soaking into my socks. I had thought I lost feeling in my hands but I felt the tingle and that familiar numbness of prolonged contact with all things winter. I could even feel the annoying tag of my shirt scratching against my neck. My hair had long since left its place behind my ear to beat at my face. Even that rhythm had stopped.

It was that pause when an arrow is pulled as far back on the bow as possible. That momentary pause before it's released.

Then the arrow flies.

It hadn't been a long recess at all but the flurry of activity that followed made everything before it seem slow.

I blinked and Dad was already almost to us. Suddenly, she was animated, lunging for him with the same level of desperation. I fell backwards, unprepared for the burst of strength from such a fragile body. She never got all the way up, stumbling forward to reach him.

He met her on his knees. She threw herself at him and, unafraid, he caught her. He supported her with both arms wrapped around her frail body. I couldn't see either of their faces. In their embrace I heard her sobbing while he soothed her.

Behind them, Liam was standing just a few feet away, breathing heavily. Ethan was at his shoulder, his eyes alternating between me and my parents. He kept his distance. It was the only way he could give my family privacy.

I didn't move from my position, undignified on the floor. I was afraid of disrupting the scene. This was no longer my world. This belonged to them. We were just spectators.

My parents pulled away just enough so they could look at each other, neither one willing to let the other go. Dad had unapologetic tears in his eyes as he searched her face. There was a smile I had never seen before.

She stopped flickering.

Her form was solidifying, as if she'd been reunited with a source of energy. She'd found a new supply of strength.

"You're here," she said to him in a voice completely present. Her eyes were so sharp and focused that she may have been unrecognizable from the woman she was before he arrived.

"*You're* here," he responded, almost laughing. The lines on his face smoothened with his smile, making him younger. He put a hand gently on her face. He didn't seem to notice that she was completely hairless or that her skin was unnaturally thin. He didn't seem to notice that she hadn't aged. He saw *her*, not the facade that defined her to the rest of the world. "How are you here?"

"I couldn't call you," she said. "I needed to keep her warm." The joy and relief that had been on her face drained away just as quickly, replaced with the look of panic I'd come to associate with her. "London," she said. "You need to take her."

"London is fine," Dad assured her. He didn't even glance my way, staring instead into her eyes and continued to caress her face. The arm around her tightened so that she couldn't break away.

She was still confused, but she trusted him completely. Evident in how her shoulders relaxed even though her expression was puzzled. She was searching for answers in his face and saw *him* for the first time.

She saw the lines that marked the passing of time. She saw the years that she had missed. She saw a man older than the one she had married. Though he didn't let her go, she leaned back a little more and put both her hands on either side of his face. His eyes closed at her touch. He only opened them again when her hands rested on his shoulders. An understanding was revealed to her in a way that eluded the rest of us.

She quickly turned her head and looked at me, finally acknowledging my presence. I saw her mouth move but I didn't hear her words. She may have whispered them or not said anything at all. Then, abruptly aware of them, she looked at Liam and Ethan. Her eyes were wide, assimilating everything around her at an accelerated pace. She returned her attention back to her husband.

"She's 17," she said to him. There was a gentle but triumphant smile on her face, her eyes alive with fierce achievement. I didn't understand how she could know that but she did. Dad nodded, almost apologetic.

"Is that young man Liam?" she asked him. Dad didn't take his eyes away from her. He was caught up in the spell of her presence and was unwilling to miss out on any of it. She was his siren, and he was listening to her song. He simply nodded again.

"Is that Lincoln?" There was additional doubt in her voice, as if she already knew the question was wrong but needed to ask it anyway.

"That's Ethan," I corrected. Finding my voice at last.

She looked at me. "Ethan," she tested the sound of his name aloud in her voice. There was approval there.

"Did you find him?" Her voice was clear, tuned, and strong. It was a summer breeze in the middle of winter, out of place but welcome. Absent the frenzy and fear, she was a completely different person. She wasn't a spectre from a nightmare. She was the woman my father had fallen in love with. She was the mother I never had. And there was more to her question than what was on the surface of it.

"In a dream," I confessed. It felt like it was the fitting thing to say. It felt like it was the correct answer to the question she was really asking.

She smiled wider. I had given her the response she was looking for. She threw her arms around Dad's neck, laughing with unrestrained joy. Her laughter rang in the air. He almost fell back from her momentum.

"You did it," she said to him over his shoulder. She was radiating with her own kind of magic.

"It was difficult without you," Dad admitted.

"You did wonderfully," she assured him. She pulled back to nestle her head on his shoulder. She was veiled in contentment that warmed her more than her faded shawl ever could.

She let the fingers of one hand trace down his chest. "I am with you in everything you do." She looked up at him, her voice filled with victorious pride. "But you didn't need me. I always knew you would be an exceptional father."

They stared at each other for a breath, sharing far more in the unbroken silence than they could with words. The unspoken communication ran deep, connecting them through combined history and constant devotion. With just a look, the years between them melted into inconsequence.

The rest of us had questions. I had so many.

My unasked questions may have been louder in my head than I thought because it somehow interrupted them. She turned her head, still on his shoulder, to look at me as if she had heard them spoken.

"There's so much I want to tell you but there isn't any time," she said. The sun was higher in the sky now, almost above the buildings. The orange, yellow glow warmed her skin in color, if not in heat. There was vitality beneath her fragile exterior.

"Are you dead?" I asked abruptly. It felt like the most pressing concern that no one was willing to address. I held my breath, bracing myself for an answer I would not like and berating myself for asking what I didn't want to know.

A single tear fell from her left eye but it was independent from her smile. That was the answer.

"I lost the ability to *cross* when I had you," she said as if what she said made any sense. "All I could do was *anchor*." She closed her eyes and settled deeper into her husband's arms. He tightened his hold on her.

"I never imagined you'd be the one to find me."

I looked at Ethan questioningly, wondering if I was the only one that could not understand what she was saying. He shook his head a fraction, a very slight and efficient motion to indicate that he was listening, even memorizing, but he couldn't follow the conversation either.

She followed my gaze but locked eyes with Liam first. "Liam," she called. "I'm so proud of you. You've done an incredible job, you know? Watching out for your father." She looked back at Dad with a tenderness that was almost tangible. "That was such a big job for a young man. You stepped up and you did so well."

Liam didn't respond, also still trying to make sense of what we all could not. He glanced at Ethan, as if to check if he was still there. Ethan wasn't looking at him because he was the next person she called. He gave her his full attention.

"Ethan," she said. "You have a responsibility that you may not yet realize but it will be your decision to embrace. It won't always be easy, but it is simple and it is worth it." He understood even less of what she said, as cryptic as it was. I could see him storing it in his head for future analysis. Now was not the time.

She looked up at the brightening sky, closed her eyes and took a deep breath, like it was the first she had taken in a long time. Then she turned back to me, a little sadder but with unmistakable optimism. "You have so many questions, I know. I wish I could answer all of them. You deserve that."

We both knew that it wasn't going to happen.

"But you'll be OK," she guaranteed. "I know you will. Just as long as you learn how to balance restraint with desire and obligation with reward. You'll find success in the middle."

Night was ending. The streetlights seemed dimmer in the increasing daylight. The sounds of traffic were louder, punctuated by a distant siren. Morning.

She touched her forehead to Dad's. "You have the best foundation ever," she continued lovingly. It was clear who she was talking about. He closed his eyes, tears streaming down his face. He kissed her.

"I'm sorry," she said to him, freely crying just the same. He shook his head, refusing to waste the moment on apologies.

"I love you," he said instead with an emphasis that carried with it many years and layers of memories. It was both forgiveness and promise. It was an oath that he never broke.

"Never enough time," she whispered in a way that indicated it had been said before and repeated often.

His laugh was short and bittersweet. "Never enough time," he echoed.

"I love you," she said, looking at him meaningfully, wanting him to understand how deep that declaration was. Wanting him to remember. They kissed again, this time with a sense of wild urgency.

At that moment, the sun broke free from the buildings that shaded it and we were all momentarily blinded.

I blinked.

When I opened my eyes, she was gone.

Dawn

Dad was holding an empty shawl in his hands.

It was clear under the light of the morning sun that there was nothing but a shawl. A mix of wind and loose snow blew through it, further highlighting her absence. The void pulsated through us with him at the epicenter.

He sat back, brought the shawl to his face and wept for the wife he had lost a second time. His shoulders shook at irregular intervals, betraying an incomprehensible pain.

I sat there for a second, still reeling from the torrents of emotion condensed in such a small window of time. I was hesitant, unsure of what my role was in this. I glanced first at Liam, who was still frozen in place, unable to level what had just happened. Then I slowly approached my grieving father.

I knelt next to him, putting a hand delicately on his back. He didn't react. I didn't want to be intrusive. I didn't want him to have the impression that I would dare presume to share even a fraction of what he was feeling. His loss was so raw and so fresh that the pain of it would define his core.

It had taken him years to find his balance. This was a hammer to an already broken heart.

I was crying too.

I don't know how long we sat there, irreverently in dirty, melting snow. Ethan had found his way next to me. I leaned my head on him just as my mother had on my father, and the reminder of it made it hard to breathe. Liam sat on the other side of Dad. His tears were silent but no less present.

Around us, unaware of what it had lost, the rest of the world continued on.

Immovable Truth

The ride back to Liam's apartment was quiet. I sat next to Dad in the backseat. Ethan had suggested it.

"He needs you," he said to me when we got back to the car.

"I don't know what to say." I felt inadequate. There was so much I wanted to give him, so much comfort I wanted to promise. Words were tissues meant to dry an ocean. Everything I could say was measly and useless.

"Then don't say anything."

We took our cues from Dad. We finally collected ourselves after he gave us one tight hug and stood up. He folded the shawl carefully, holding it in his arms like it was crystal. His eyes were sore and tired, heavy but dry. Emptied.

Everything we did felt mechanical. We functioned out of habit and expectation without processing purpose.

Get in the car. Drive home. Shower. Cry. Sleep.

That was the plan. No one talked about it but it was the agenda we were all following.

I leaned against Dad, not saying anything as Ethan suggested but also letting him know I was there. Hoping he could take what he needed from that.

His smile was tight and small, a fragment of what it was in her presence. It was acknowledgment of my attempt and I found that I was grateful. I was the one that was supposed to be comforting him, but he was the one making me feel better. Classic. He was selflessly providing for his children even when he was beaten and shattered.

He sacrificed over and over again. He hid the dents and missing armor and took the brunt of the unfairness of the world. And when he found his reward for all his trails, the universe mocked him and took that away too. It was not just unfair; it was cruel.

I only realized I was crying again when I felt it down my chin. I sat up and wiped my face roughly with the back of my sleeve. I wasn't supporting him. I wasn't helping him. I was failing.

You had one job, London.

Dad had Mom's shawl cradled on his lap. He took one hand away from it and laid it over mine. *You have the best foundation ever*, she had said. He proved it again and again.

"I'm sorry, Dad," I said just over a whisper, breaking the silence. There was no apology that could summarize all my regret and desire to relieve him of all this heartbreak. "It's just so unfair."

He didn't respond right away, nor did I expect him to. I was venting, not making conversation. It sounded juvenile and didn't do justice to the consuming emotions that demanded to be identified. The thought that this was infinitely more painful to him only angered me more. It was a downward spiral that multiplied as it continued. I couldn't find redemption.

When he spoke, it was without the outrage I was feeling. The sadness hadn't been erased but there was something else that steadied it. "Thank you," he said in a voice that I'd never heard before.

"Sweetheart," he continued, "*I'm* sorry. I didn't trust you the way you deserved. You are your mother's daughter and I should have supported your instincts even when they sounded outrageous." His own words made him smile a little wider, contrary to the shine in his eyes that hinted at tears. "Don't quote me on this but I'm grateful you didn't listen to me. I'm grateful that you are the young woman that you are, finding your path and way to get there."

It was not at all what I expected.

"You're not … angry with me?" He obviously wasn't but it surprised me how far he was in the opposite direction that I voiced it out anyway.

He should be angry. He should be resentful. I was.

He shook his head. "How can I be? You led me back to her."

"All for nothing." I could actually taste the bitterness in my voice. I should be fostering his acceptance, but instead I was pulling him along my descending vortex.

"Oh, Sweetheart." The way he said that caught my attention. It was the tone he used right before he would reveal the solution to a tricky math problem. It was the tone he used when he knew the answer to *Clue* before anyone else did. Partly pleased with himself and also eager to be the one to reveal it.

We had arrived at different conclusions and I wasn't seeing what was so obvious to him.

"This was *everything*," he emphasized. "You did this. Because of you, I was given another chance."

I was confused by his joy. It was the antithesis of what I was feeling. "But, she couldn't stay." I was stating what I thought was obvious because it seemed like he was missing it.

He looked down at the shawl, still damp from melted snow, and caressed it like he had her face. "It was never about making her stay, Sweetheart."

"You barely had time," I argued, still indignant for what was taken away.

His smile was replaced with more gravity, comparable to the weight of his words. He wanted to cut through my resentment. "It's not always about the amount of time you have. It's about what you do with what you're given."

It was a simple observation that hit me harder than what I was prepared for. It was what Ethan had been trying to tell me. I had refused to hear it. I was selfishly and foolishly wasting my moments complaining about the unfairness of not having more. I was envious of others when I should have recognized what I had.

I had to witness my father's pain to understand.

"I wasn't cheated, Sweetheart. I was rewarded." What I had mistaken for emptiness was a tired kind of peace. He was so blissful in her presence that anything less seemed like defeat. But that really wasn't the case. She had left something with him, a tranquility of sorts. I was too caught up in my own drama to see it.

"You gave me another chance to hear her voice. Another chance to hold her." He closed his eyes, back in the memory of having her in his arms and basking in it. "Another chance to tell her I loved her."

His smile was back, tempered but true. "In those few moments, I was able to love her for another lifetime." His was a better tribute to her than anger. It was a more appropriate homage than bitterness. "It is immeasurably more than what I had before and it is more than what most people will get."

His wisdom in the wake of such devastation crashed into me in a wave of sudden cognizance. I should have been carried away with the shame of my stupidity. Instead, I was anchored to one immovable truth.

Love transcends time.

Ethan had been right and I could finally see it. The only influence time has over love is to strengthen it. Otherwise, it has no authority. I've had the privilege of witnessing it all my life without the maturity to recognize it. Realizing my ignorance made me feel that much smaller and insignificant. How could I have remained so oblivious?

There, in a hushed reverence of what had transpired, did I ultimately learn how to never underestimate the power of love.

Chapter One

Drew and Brieann were waiting outside the house. It was starting to get dark already but they looked comfortable sitting together on the front steps. Drew had his elbows on the step behind them, one arm behind Brieann in a casual but intimate way. I had texted them when we landed in Sacramento; so they knew when we'd be back.

"This is new," I said to Ethan. Dad was pulling into the driveway, and I saw Ethan look out the window as we passed. Seeing how everything in this foreign country was still fairly new to him, he wasn't sure what I was commenting on. I noticed that only Drew's car was by the curb. Brieann did not take her own.

The weekend in Chicago had been pivotal. We didn't really talk about what happened again. We didn't bring it up with Chase when we met up with him and Philip for dinner. He had been surprised to see us, and Dad made it seem like it had been his idea to fly in for the weekend.

We spent the rest of the time healing by sharing stories and laughing more than we cried. We made new memories, embracing all the opportunities. Chase even got Ethan and me tickets to watch *The Blue Man Group*. We ate the candy I had meant to use as bribes. These were all real experiences that I will always have to hold.

By the time we were on the flight back, we were all physically and emotionally spent but our hearts were significantly lighter.

When my friends found out that Dad was also in Chicago and he had not killed me, or worse, taken my phone away, they were reassured. Then they started sending a series of pictures that they entitled *Living on the Edge: A Weekend With Uncle Drew*.

It consisted of pictures of Ethan's knife under the supervision of Drew. The first night, we received a picture of his knife tucked into its own bed made of a used Amazon box and an old pillowcase. In the morning it was his knife next to a bowl of *Lucky Charms*. By the afternoon, his knife apparently had visited the park, painted a picture, had ice cream, and binge-watched *Supernatural*. Ethan almost jumped an earlier flight to rescue his property.

"Hand it over." Ethan got to Drew before I could. The growl was a friendly threat. It would have been more menacing but Ethan had learned moderation when he had started Boot Camp recently. Fortunately for Drew.

Drew grinned. It was obvious what Ethan was talking about and he didn't act like he didn't know. He dug into the front of his jeans pocket and retrieved the knife. "But we were going to start Season Four tonight," Drew protested. "That's when it really gets good." Despite his claims, he offered the knife back to Ethan without dispute.

Ethan swiped it out of Drew's hand with force but the wry smile betrayed his positive mood. The street lights had just come on as they did every evening at dark. The artificial light reflected against the blade when he flipped it open. He grinned at the sound of the familiar clack. Then he let it loose. It danced around his hand faster than usual, spinning in the air so that the knife edge flashed in the light. We could hear the air being cut. He was showing off. Drew and Brieann took a step back.

"OK, Psycho." I said, rolling my eyes. "Your testosterone-filled point has been made." Ethan caught the knife in midair and pocketed it. He looked supremely pleased with himself.

I would deny it, but there was always something with how he handled that knife that was just so attractive. Maybe it was the danger that he so masterfully controlled. Maybe it was more primal. I couldn't explain it; so it was just easier to pretend otherwise. As long as no one called me out on it.

With the deadly weapon safely stored, Brieann threw herself at me, embracing me with more enthusiasm than I was ready for. High-pitched squeals were involved. I returned the hug and realized that I had wanted it just as much. Another thing that I would likely deny.

"I'm so glad you're OK," she said too close to my ear.

"Me too," I said. And I meant it.

When she let go, I cleared my throat and decided I would rather talk about them than myself. I've had enough introspection for the weekend. "What's going on here?" I made motions between the two of them with my fingers.

Brieann shared a shy look with Drew and actually blushed. She lowered her chin demurely but her eyes were on fire. I was enjoying this. This was the same kind of power she had over me when we talked about Ethan. I understood the allure.

Drew, on the other hand, pulled himself a little taller. Grinning, he put an arm around her and kissed her high on her cheek. A small demonstration that confirmed my suspicion. She didn't look like she minded at all.

"We bonded over your fate," Drew said. Brieann laughed. It was a laughter born of genuine delight.

"Oh, Brieann," I said, taking both her hands and dragging her away from Drew. "I'm so sorry." She laughed again.

"Hey!" Drew protested. He reached for her hand, but I pulled her away before he could reach her.

"I didn't mean for this to happen!" I yelled at her, pushing her the other direction. "Run! Run! Save yourself!"

She did not run. Still laughing, she turned around and stood next to Drew. "I was told there was a 30-day trial period," she said, teasing him. Drew pretended to be hurt but there was too much cheer for him to hide.

I laughed. That sounded like Drew. "That's how they get you," I warned her. "Always read the fine print."

"There is no fine print," Drew claimed. "What you see is what you get." He put his arm around her shoulders and she put one around his waist. They fit well together. Peanut butter and jelly. Grilled cheese and tomato soup.

Peas in a pod.

"Again," I said to Brieann. "I'm so sorry." But I was grinning wildly.

Brieann was enjoying the banter. Drew fixed me with a glare too exaggerated to be real. Adorable. I hugged them both at once, forcing them in odd, uncomfortable positions. "I'm kidding, of course. I love this! This is perfect!"

I squealed between the two of them. The roles have been reversed and I was now the one screaming in their ears. I pulled them together more tightly and they were laughing in the midst of protests.

"You guys are great together," I said, letting them go. Drew acted like he was recovering from a choke slam and Brieann re-tied her hair up in one fluid, expert motion.

"That's what I told her," Drew said. He reached for her hand. She met him half way and squeezed. It was a little gesture but behind it was a more meaningful expression. I saw it and I could appreciate it.

"And she actually believed you."

"I can be persuasive," he responded, acting hurt. Brieann's broad smile meant that he didn't have to push too hard to convince her.

"I figured," she said, "that I'd rather spend my last year in high school with people I actually like being with. Those are the memories worth having. Everything else is just so exhausting."

"She gave up her popularity for me," Drew laughed, both hands over his heart. "Isn't that romantic?" She bumped his hip with hers playfully. "I'm not giving up anything," she protested, lifting her chin in defiance. "I'm gaining something."

"You're going to start hanging out with the likes of me," he reminded her. "Mere riffraff." He held his cupped hands out like a Charles Dickens orphan. "Please, miss," he said in a tiny voice. "May I have some attention?" The theater kid in him was enjoying all the characters he was acting out.

"She started hanging out with me first," I reminded him. "The damage was already done there."

"'Tis true," Drew said at the exact same time Brieann was protesting.

The laughter felt right. I shared a smile with Ethan, who put his arm around my shoulder. I leaned against him, enjoying his warmth.

"Do your friends want to stay for dinner?" Dad called from the front door. I looked first at him, appreciating how much more at peace he seemed with himself. There was contentment that I hadn't seen before. Then I looked back at said friends. Brieann nodded and Drew shrugged.

"That sounds super, Dr. Evans," Drew said, accepting the invitation for both himself and Brieann as a unit.

"We don't have dinner," I reminded Dad, tensing up. The weekend had been a hot mess. I couldn't remember what we had stored in the fridge. We might have a jar of pickles. Or several cans of beans. Dad wasn't bothered.

"There's always pizza," he responded wisely. It wasn't the actual food that was important. It was the company. He was right. I relaxed.

"There's always pizza," I agreed with both the cuisine as well as the sentiment.

"Call it in already," he ordered. "It's dinnertime and I'm hungry." He turned his back on us, leading the way inside the house. "I don't know about you kids but I'll be inside where it's warm."

He had a point. There wasn't any snow and I still had my thick hoodie, but I felt the chill on my hands and ears. "Yeah," I agreed. "Let's take this inside."

Drew made sure his car was locked before offering a crooked arm for Brieann to take. She hooked her arm playfully with his and they walked up the steps, their heads close together with shared familiarity.

Their relationship was beginning a phase that they were both equally enthusiastic to discover together. Things would be different among all of us, but I realized I was looking forward to it.

"That's what you meant by something new," Ethan said to me when they were out of earshot. "How did you know?"

I looked up at him, seeing him silhouetted against the light. The contrast made it a little difficult for my eyes to adjust but I waited until I could see him more clearly. The tightness between his brows had eased. The tension he was carrying when we started this whole adventure had finally faded. His eyes were the perfect balance of green and gold.

"They looked at each other differently," I said, knowing that I looked at him the same way. "Love helps you see someone how they were meant to be seen, how they deserve to be seen. They see each other now." He smiled and I wondered what he saw when he looked at me.

"Thank you," I said again. I've said it many times but the frequency had not diluted the significance of the words. "I know everything has been so crazy lately."

He looked at me incredulously a half -second before bursting into laughter. "Lately?" he repeated. "You do recall that I met you out in the *wop-wops* and that you disappeared into thin air when you were hit by a lorry, yeah?"

"*Almost* hit," I corrected him, but I conceded his valid argument.

"Our relationship began with you thinking that I was a figment of your imagination," he pointed out. He wasn't finished yet. "And you thought that I thought that you were an *alien*!"

I had to laugh. He wasn't wrong. And those were only the first of many examples he could list. He pulled me to face him in a close hug. "*Everything* about this is mental, yeah," he emphasized. "But everything about you is magical."

We didn't say anything right away, just enjoyed that quiet communion. How quickly he had become a beacon in my life. He was the point of origin I can always return to. He was my center. I had almost lost him and I had been so afraid that it would happen again. I was afraid that our relationship, borne under such extreme and unlikely circumstances, would be too feeble to endure something as mundane as distance.

And, if that happened, I was afraid of having to continue alone.

"After having this," I said, wrapping both my arms around him and laying my head on his chest. "How are we going to be satisfied with emails and video calls?"

I complained but I wasn't so afraid anymore. I learned that between us, we had the power to overcome worldly obstacles. I learned that while there are many ugly and scary hurdles to worry about, we were stronger than that. And if we weren't yet, we can be.

He lifted my chin so that I would look at him.

"It won't always be easy," he started to say, leaning down to me. "But it is simple." His lips brushed mine, a preamble to a kiss. I recognized the words but they sounded different in his voice. He paused and I felt his smile. "And it is, unequivocally, worth it."

The kiss that finally followed was testament to that.

Above us, the sky had started to darken but the faint stars twinkled with the promise of reward.

Thank You

This Old Book
Providing new life to old books and attention to the new smaller ones.

Grayslake Area Public Library
Home of my very first Author Visit.

Local libraries
Giving a new writer a chance.

Lorenz Laureola
Spending your birthday reading Reverie. Also all the plot suggestions that I will never use and will unlikely forget.

Bel Laureola
Making Lorenz buy more copies and encouraging others to do the same.

Logene Laureola
The memes. So. Many. Memes.

Jason DeGuzman
Being the brother to me that completed the set. And liking every single post on social media about Reverie.

Peggy Lacson
Being the bonus mom I didn't know I was missing.

Victor Lacson
Teaching me all about the yabang factor.

Kari Pohar
Proving that community is stronger than competition and friendship makes the best stories.

Marianne Ambrose
Purchasing multiple copies of the same book and multiple candles that you will never burn.

Kari Fitzgerald
My dependable co-host for our non-existent weekly food blogs. We probably wouldn't be talking about food.

Ellie MacKellar
Eyeballing the advanced copy of Revenant.

Jill Elicaño Tan
The mysterious ways you're able to obtain a copy of Reverie from the other side of the world before anyone else in the county.

Dana McDonald
You really should stop talking to strangers on the Internet now.

Julie Reiner & Jamie Vanderwarker
These women almost kept me from finishing this book by making me count to 100 repeatedly.

Beth McGowan
I owe it to her to get her name right at some point.

The Grayslake Area Public Library Writer's Group
Cheering along every milestone and being a resource for all local aspiring authors.

The Grayslake Arts Alliance
Fostering an environment of supportive artists.

David Rutter
I would not have considered doing a second book had you not insisted that I should.

Woolgatherers Around The World
Dreaming and making my dreams come true.

About the Author

ZEE LACSON

Zee was born and raised in Manila, Philippines. She grew up with her dad, brothers, and grandparents. She lives in the North Suburbs of Chicagoland, IL with her husband, twin sons and a fluffy dog that often interrupts her process.

She is an engineer by education, a photographer by profession, an artist by practice, and a writer by soul.

She drinks good coffee and appreciates fresh sushi. Just not together.

Revenant is her second published work of fiction.

Reverie was her first.

CPSIA information can be obtained
at www.ICGtesting.com
Printed in the USA
LVHW081445090721
692105LV00020BA/1295